COWBOY RANSOM

BARB HAN

TORJAKE PUBLISHING

To my family for unwavering love and support. I can't imagine doing life with anyone else. I love you guys with all my heart.

Coby McGannon stopped cold. He'd walked down this same aisle at Feed and Seed countless times over the years and never once had someone caught his eye or had his pulse race like a school kid.

Even Diesel, his four-legged faithful companion, seemed to catch onto the shift in the air. The dog stared up at Coby with quite the confused expression.

An impulse struck to go talk to the leggy blonde with silky ash hair cascading over her shoulders. Her back was turned to him, but she must be new in town. There was no way he would have missed her if he'd seen her before. Her teal green off the shoulder dress fell mid-thigh, exposing long legs that were tucked into a pair of custom boots. The boots were brown with delicate white flowers etched in them. A belt cinched at her waistline showed off her figure

She wasn't tall, coming in at five-foot-two-inches if he had to venture a guess. So, basically, she was all legs— creamy skin and...

He stopped himself right there. Had it really come to this? Gawking at the first attractive unattached woman he came across? He hoped she was single. He didn't have a clear view of her ring finger. And, granted, he hadn't been on a date in too long, but that was no excuse. Considering everything going on with his family after his uncle's 'accident' and his father's subsequent arrest his mind had been pre-occupied. Dating was the last thing on his mind.

He'd been picking up slack for one person or another at the ranch more than usual, not that he minded. Plus, two of his brothers had up and walked out to start a taco truck business. Coby suspected they were tired of the drama that had been stretching on for too many months at the family's successful cattle ranch. It was getting to him too.

Clearly. He was standing in the middle of Feed and Seed staring at a stranger. The thought of the mystery woman turning toward him, busting him, got his feet moving in the opposite direction. Diesel followed.

Diesel was the best dog Coby had ever known, one hundred and thirty-five pounds of solid muscle, loyalty, and devotion. Having been dumped 'in the country' when he was barely weaned from his mother, Coby had rescued him before any permanent emotional damage had set in. Since Coby was all the dog knew as family, his loyalty had no bounds. They were inseparable, save for Diesel's occasional desire to stick around the barn for a day, and Coby wouldn't have it any other way.

He ran a mental checklist, focusing on his shopping list and the reason he'd driven to the store in the first place. He had a new pair of gloves and the heartworm medicine in hand. He could check those off the list.

As soon as he'd walked in the front door, Mick had nodded and waved. He would have Diesel's food in a cart waiting at checkout. Personal service was one of the many reasons he preferred shopping at the feed store versus doing his shopping online. Plus, he liked to support local businesses. Feed and Seed delivered, but his order wasn't big enough to warrant a special trip. Plus, he and Diesel had to pass by on their way home from their favorite fishing spot. Sunday mornings in the fall were for fishing. Coby almost laughed out loud because he probably smelled like he'd had his hands stuck in a fish's mouth too, not that he'd caught any worth keeping. Another reason to hightail it the opposite way of Legs over there before she caught a whiff and ran in the opposite direction to get away from him.

He could admit that a big part of him was curious about her. Who was she? Where did she live? Why was she in town and for how long? If she was passing through, he didn't really need to waste his time. If by some stroke of luck she was sticking around, it would be difficult to hide in a town this size where everyone knew each other's business. At some point, he'd run into her again.

Patience. That was a word Coby understood.

"Hey, Mick." Coby acknowledged the owner. The man was average height. His build could best be described as wiry. He had a full head of white hair and amazing strength for a man of fifty-plus years. He could out bench press guys half his age if we wanted to and was always quick to hop on a truck bed and load up whatever supplies a customer needed help with. His enthusiasm made him a favorite in Cattle Cove.

"What are you up to today?" Mick asked as he punched codes into the register. He put a hand up momentarily as if to stop Coby from spilling the beans. "No, wait. It's Sunday." He took a sniff in Coby's direction. "You've been to the quarry. What did you catch?"

Coby gave a quick update on the state of his fishing as the older gentlemen finished ringing him up, nodding in appreciation at each of Coby's catches. Mick grabbed a treat from the container sitting on top of the counter and came around to say hello to Diesel.

"How's this guy today?" Mick's treat was basically licked off the flat of his palm.

"He's as ornery as ever. Ended up in a burr patch that cost me a trout because I couldn't stand for him to suffer for even a second."

"Better than a skunk," Mick quipped with a wink.

"He's done that before too." Coby laughed. He started to ask about Legs back there but decided against it. He hadn't thought to look for a ring and it wasn't polite to ask about someone who might already be spoken for. It wasn't polite to gawk at her either, an annoying voice in his head pointed out.

He silenced that pain in the neck real quick.

Mick gave Diesel a good head scratch and the dog ate up the attention. There were times when Coby would swear the animal was smiling. This was one of them.

"You're a good boy, aren't you," Mick practically cooed before rounding back to the cash register and finishing the sales transaction. He nodded toward the cart. "Need any help out with that?"

"No, thanks. I got it." Coby wheeled the cart outside and toward his Jeep that was parked in the back of the lot. Several vehicles had cleared out, making it easy to identify the few remaining. There was one he recognized four cars and one aisle over as Sheriff Laney Justice's personal vehicle.

At least he didn't run into her today. To say things had become awkward after she'd arrested his father for attempted murder was an understatement. What could he say? His family life was complicated and she was at the center of it lately. The conversation he needed to have with her about when his father would be released since making bail could wait. This was Sunday, a day he tried to unplug from all the stress; not invite more in.

Coby cursed at the piece of paper stuck to his windshield as he pushed the cart behind his vehicle. He tossed all four fifty-pound bags in the back along with the gloves and heartworm medication, securing the latter in a side compartment meant for just such items.

Flyers were one of the biggest annoyances known to man. He stalked around the vehicle to snatch this one off his Jeep. He couldn't have been in the feed store more than fifteen minutes. Someone had worked fast to be able to put these on all the vehicles without being caught.

As he glanced around to see if he could find the culprit, he realized no one else had flyers. How did he end up the lone lucky jerk?

He issued a sharp sigh, thinking it was always a pain to deal with these as he snatched the piece of paper off his windshield. Diesel hopped into the passenger seat, like he always did, ready and waiting.

"I'll be over in a second," Coby muttered under his breath.

He never knew what to do with these advertisements. Chunking them on the ground was just littering. It wasn't Mick's fault his customers' vehicles occasionally got bombed with one of these, especially as he'd already politely called a few businesses who thought it was all right to blast Mick's customers and fill his parking lot with litter. Coby normally wadded the flyers up and chunked them in the trash once he got home, even though he hated bringing them all the way to the ranch.

He smoothed out the edge against the window of his

Jeep. The handwriting caught his attention. Weren't these advertisements normally computer generated?

Coby squinted against the bright sun to get a better look at the writing. His pulse kicked up a couple of notches. He glanced around to see if anyone was standing nearby, watching. A cold chill raced down his back as he took a second look at the threatening note.

He smoothed out the rest of the page and kept reading. Granted, a lot had been going on recently, and his family was at the center of most of the crime wave for reasons he had yet to figure out. No way could this message be meant for him. Right? This note had to be on the wrong vehicle, a case of mistaken identity.

Mother and baby don't have to die. Ur choice. The message referenced a woman and a baby. Coby had neither in his life. More proof this note couldn't be intended for him.

Look for cell. No calls. Text only.

Coby glanced around the outside of his vehicle and saw nothing. Nothing on the hood or dashboard. He moved to the driver's side and immediately caught sight of a sliver of silver on his seat. How had he missed it? He'd been too concerned and frustrated with getting the piece of paper off his windshield.

He surveyed the parking lot to see if there were any suspicious-looking vehicles around. Was this even real? Couldn't be. His mind snapped to this being some kind of terrible joke. No one he knew would pull something like this, and yet the note couldn't possibly be aimed at him. A case of mistaken identity?

Frustration nailed his gut. From what he could gather, a woman and her baby had been kidnapped. This was a ransom note. Half a million dollars for the baby and a quarter of a million for the woman. Each delivered separately like some kind of Amazon package.

Another thought struck. Could this note have been meant for someone else in his family? One of his brothers? Cousins? There were no babies in the mix that he knew of. Still, he fished his own cell phone out of his pocket and made a quick call to his brother Reed.

"Everyone okay at the ranch?" he asked his oldest brother before Reed had a chance to speak.

"As far as I know. Why?" Reed's curiosity was understandable. Coby's call was coming out of the blue.

"Checking in with everyone." The last couple of lines on the note kept him from explaining. *Bring anyone else into this and the woman dies. Tell the sheriff and the baby goes with her mother.*

"I haven't heard anything," Reed confirmed.

"Is anyone acting strangely today?" Coby pressed.

"Not that I've seen but I haven't been around everyone. Why?" Reed's voice hitched on the last word. His concern came through heavy on the line.

"Thanks. Don't worry. I'll explain everything later." There would be more questions leaving the conversation on this note. Coby hated leaving his brother in the dark, even though it couldn't be helped. "I have a few other calls to make and not a whole lot of time. I'll circle back."

"Okay." Reed drew out the word.

Coby ended the call promising to catch his brother up as soon as he could. It took a solid ten minutes to confirm everyone's whereabouts. Coby breathed a sigh of relief after ending the last call. He leaned against his Jeep, wondering if he should take the bait and pick up the cell phone in his driver's seat.

As he glanced up, he caught sight of Legs walking one

aisle over, heading straight for...

Hold on. It couldn't be. *No. No. No.*

This couldn't be happening. Not when his day had already taken a serious turn for the worse. The woman he'd been pining for couldn't be her. Just couldn't be. He could almost hear the universe laughing at him this very minute because Legs was none other than Sheriff Laney Justice in plain clothes. Could this day get any worse?

Never mind. He took those words back because as bad as it felt lately, and bad was an understatement, things could always go further south.

The fact he hadn't recognized Laney from behind shouldn't be too shocking. He'd never made an effort to look at her 'behind' before.

Coby ducked his head down a little too late because she abandoned her cart and started heading straight for him. He bit back a curse. What the heck was he supposed to do with the paper in his hand? If she saw it, game over. Lives could be in jeopardy. He couldn't exactly hide it behind his back, like a six-year-old getting caught with candy in his hands before supper.

So, he acted casual, crossing his legs at his ankles.

"Sheriff," he said as she approached.

"Coby," she flashed those light green eyes of hers at him. Those, he'd noticed before. Her eyes were the most unusual shade of light green. The color of the dress brought her irises out even more. "I hope it's okay if I call you by your first name."

"Yes, ma'am," he was being intentionally formal with her.

"Please, call me Laney," she said.

Getting on a personal level with Laney Justice was probably a bad idea after the thoughts he'd had in the feed store.

She'd always been pretty, even with her hair pulled back in a bun and tucked underneath a hat most of the time. Sunglasses normally shaded her eyes and, in all honesty, he did his level best to avoid her when she visited the main house.

"Everything all right over here?" Her eyebrow arched.

He could play this scenario one of two ways. The first would be to cover up what was going on and wish Sheriff... Laney...a good day. The second would be to come clean about what he found on his vehicle and risk getting caught by the person who placed it there. The saying *caught between a rock and a hard place* came to mind. On the one hand, involving law enforcement could anger the perp and cost two lives. On the other, not involving someone with experience and training could cost two lives and possibly his own if he made a misstep.

"What's that in your hand?" Her curiosity must have gotten the better of her as she nodded toward the evidence.

This situation was serious. Deadly? Coby had no training in law enforcement or kidnappings. He didn't know what to ask for or when. And there were possibly two lives on the line, none of whom he was related to but that didn't mean he didn't care or feel the weight of responsibility on his chest. Weight that felt like a truck had docked on his chest.

When he didn't immediately answer, she shifted her weight from one foot to the other and repeated her question. "Is everything okay?"

"Fine."

"I'm not the enemy, Coby. I want the truth of what happened that day too." She thought he was concerned about the case involving his father? He was, in the broader sense. Just not in this moment.

He weighed his options. If he didn't tell her and someone died because he made a mistake, he wouldn't be able to live with himself. If he involved her and someone died because of his actions, he wouldn't be able to live with himself. Trying to handle this on his own would be stupid. There were so many ways he could be tricked. Plus, he needed help figuring out who this message was intended for.

Since he had zero law enforcement experience and, if he believed the note, lives were at stake, there was no real choice.

"This isn't about Donny's case." He glanced around to make sure no one was watching before tilting the note toward her so she could read it.

Those intelligent and beautiful green eyes widened as she stared at the page. "This is serious."

"I'm aware."

"I mean it," she shot back.

"So do I. In fact, I almost didn't show you because of the last lines. I'm in over my head here and I have no idea what my next move should be," he admitted.

"I need to bring in—"

"No one else gets involved. I'm not risking it. Now, I could use your help but you can't breathe a word of this to anyone." He stopped there when he heard how that must sound. She wasn't one to take orders.

Laney's eyebrow shot up, making him very aware she would be the one calling the shots here. She blinked up at him with concern in her eyes, clearly evaluating options too.

"Who is she?" she finally asked.

"No idea." He shrugged. "I don't have a child and there's no one special in my life."

2

Laney Justice stared into the most golden pair of brown eyes she'd ever seen. Of course, Coby McGannon was six-feet-five-inches so she wasn't exactly eye-to-eye with him. A trill of awareness skittered across her skin. Wholly inappropriate under the circumstances. And yet, her body reacted to his strong male presence anyway.

She studied him for a long moment after re-reading the letter. She believed him when he said he had no idea who'd placed the note on his Jeep, and this wasn't the time or place to exhale her relief at the admission he wasn't attached to anyone at the moment. His relationship status was none of her business if it didn't impact this case. She needed to get a grip.

"What if someone put this note on the wrong vehicle?" he asked. "I almost crumpled it up and tossed it in the backseat so I could take it home and throw it away."

"You would have noticed the cell phone," she pointed out.

He nodded before his lips formed a grim line. "There's

going to be a timer. If I fail at any point, the baby will die first."

Laney studied the note. Sure enough, what Coby said was true.

"I already asked this but it's important to try and establish a connection to you or your family. Is there a possibility the child is yours?"

"There's always a possibility. I'm not celibate, but I use protection every time whether someone I'm involved with is on the pill or using any other type of birth control. It's non-negotiable." He'd crossed his arms over his chest in a show of feeling exposed. His legs were crossed at the ankles. His body language said he didn't really want to be talking about his sex life with her. He didn't strike her as the kiss and tell type either.

Fair but this conversation was necessary to the case. She needed to first establish if there was any possible connection between him and the victims. Right now, they had a note, a cell phone, and an unidentified perp's word harm would come to others if Coby didn't cooperate.

"Can we go somewhere private and talk?" He took his time surveying the area.

Her office was out. There was no way he would agree to going there. Public places were out, since they had no idea who'd placed the note on his Jeep and if the perp could be watching right now. She had her laptop at home and could access the work database there to see if any similar crimes had been committed in the area or the state.

"My house isn't far from here." She glanced around too.

"Text me your address and I'll meet you there."

"Okay, then. Be careful with the piece of paper. I'll dust it for prints later when we're out of sight." She walked back to her sedan, watching for any movement or anyone who might be a little too interested in her or Coby's activities. Her pulse pounded, which wasn't unusual when she got a new case. This time was different. More intense. More erratic. More everything.

Did Coby have something to do with the change? The air charged around her when she'd been standing close enough to him to read the ransom note.

He had teddy-bear soft eyes and they were the only soft things on a face of hard angles and sharp planes. The term 'made from granite' applied to his jawline, and probably his muscles too. His body looked sculpted in a gym but she knew he'd earned every muscle working on his family's ranch. And despite being one of the wealthiest cattle ranching families in the state, he was the most down-to-earth person. All the McGannons were that way. It was just the way they were built.

They had other good qualities she didn't want to dwell on while she hopped in the driver's seat and then fired off a text. He peeled out of the parking lot, making a show of his exit and she figured that was in case anyone was watching.

Coby was smart. It was a good move. She also realized he had extensive experience tracking poachers on his family's land. Poachers were some of the most dangerous criminals in Texas and were real threats to cattle families. The McGannons rarely called in for help. The call usually came in once they'd detained a violator and were ready for the person to be picked up and jailed. In fact, the family was notoriously private, so her investigation into his father had to be an intrusion no one appreciated, despite everyone cooperating.

Donny McGannon had been bad news since his arrival in town. He'd cashed out his inheritance and ditched his sons years ago, leaving them for his brother to raise. He was opposite his brother and sons in every notable way, and still under investigation for attempting to murder his brother despite making bail. She exhaled the breath she didn't realize she'd been holding and started up her engine.

Making certain no one followed her out of the parking lot, she took a detour home from her normal route. It took twice as long but driving around Main Street and through town was the best way to ensure no one followed.

When she was satisfied, she turned onto Aster Circle and pulled onto the portico. She parked smack in front of her home and searched for Coby's Jeep. Had he given up and gone home? Or was he driving around, giving her plenty of time to get to her place first?

She checked her cell. No message.

Laney grabbed her handbag and bag of cat supplies. There was a feral kitten that she'd spotted in her backyard looking for a meal; she'd put out a can of tuna and the kitten had eaten like she hadn't had a bite in days. Laney wanted to keep putting out a bowl with food in case the little tabby came back.

Of course, in this town, it was just as likely a raccoon or armadillo would clean out the food, which was why Laney decided to bring in the bowl at night to remove temptation from unwanted visitors.

She put her key in the door, pausing long enough to take another look around. She dismissed the thought Coby might have changed his mind about including her. He was smart enough to know that could spell disaster and he wouldn't want that on his conscience anyway.

The door caught. She shouldered it open before closing and locking it. There was a time not that long ago when she wouldn't think twice about leaving her front door unlocked. Heck, she would have left her keys in her vehicle while she ran into the store too. She might have even left her engine running.

Times had changed.

She stepped into the living room and nearly jumped out of her skin. "How did you get in my house?"

Coby was sitting on the sofa with the note next to him. His teddy bear eyes were intent on the message. "I let myself in."

Well, him and his dog were in her living room. And did she smell fish?

"How?" she demanded, thinking the wind must have taken the odor in the opposite direction when they were outside earlier. Inside these four walls, it was strong enough to draw all the neighborhood cats in.

"You have a key under the houseplant in your screened-in patio in back. You leave it there for company, right?" He glanced up and her heart squeezed. The man was billboard model good looking despite the fishy smell.

"Yes." The word came out as a croak, her throat suddenly dry. She swallowed to ease the dryness, like that did any good. "It's for invited guests to use."

Those brown eyes stared at her and a dark brow went up. "I thought I *was* invited."

The McGannon charm was legendary. Seeing it in full force helped her understand why. There was something about a tall, gorgeous cowboy who would see chivalry as his duty that disarmed a person, even her. Didn't mean she had to let him get away with it.

"Is that fish I smell?" On her white couch?

"Sorry." He pushed to standing and put his hands out, palms up, in the surrender position. "Where would you have me set up?"

"Over there. The kitchen table. I work there sometimes."

The two-bedroom bungalow had been opened up with a modernized floorplan. The place was small, cozy and perfect for one person. She had a second bedroom that was set up for guests. Rarely used, but ready to go at a moment's notice. Or, at least, rarely used in recent months because her caseload had been keeping her insanely busy. It was strange how so many of her contemporaries left Cattle Cove for greener pastures. Or, to be more factual, the city. She understood on some level. There wasn't a variety of jobs available in this town that was mostly made up of cattle ranchers and a small, close-knit community of family-owned businesses. She also got that it wasn't always great to stay in a town where people had long memories. She'd never lived down hers from middle school when she was the first to raise her hand in almost every class. Brainy Laney had been born on the playground, thanks to Tommy Landon. The name had stuck and she still got the occasional snicker behind her back when someone didn't think she could hear them. She could.

There were worse nicknames she could have been stuck with, so she gritted her teeth and smiled anyway. Since she'd been a couple of grades ahead of Coby in school, she prayed he hadn't heard the name. It shouldn't matter to her and caught her off guard that it did.

A couple of years seemed like a huge age gap in high school. A freshman rarely ever dated a junior or senior. Now, later in life, a couple of years was a drop in the bucket. Funny how perspective changed with experience.

She grabbed her laptop from the desk in her bedroom and toed off her boots. When she returned to the living room, Diesel was curled up in the middle of the floor situated near Coby but also where he could get a good look in all directions. His protective instincts were strong. She'd rarely ever seen the two of them apart out on the land. Inside the main house was a different story, but he rarely spent time in there. Had it always been like that? Or was that new?

She grabbed a seat across the table from Coby, thinking she also needed to open a window and turn on a fan both because he was hotness on a stick and the fish smell in equal measure. She booted up her laptop before grabbing a fingerprinting kit. Paper was always difficult. Wouldn't stop her from trying, though.

"Did you bring the cell phone they left behind in your vehicle?" she asked.

"Yes, and I did my best not to leave a print."

"Good. Maybe we'll be able to lift something and get a name from the database." It was probably too much to hope but sometimes criminals got in a hurry and missed a critical piece. All it took was one mistake to blow a case wide open. She'd seen it happen too many times to count it out. Those cases solved themselves. There were a lot of moving parts to committing a crime. Overlooking one aspect could be the difference between freedom and jail time. Of course, she would be able to start putting together a picture of the perp based on the decisions he'd made so far and how well he covered his tracks. Basics, like if he was a career criminal or someone going for a quick money grab.

A quick snatch-and-grab-for-a-fast-buck perp would most likely be inexperienced and the easiest to catch. A pro would be a whole different ballgame.

She studied the note again before dusting it for prints. She needed more to go on before she could make a determination about this perp's experience.

Once she was done, she bagged up the kit and set it on the table by the front door where she kept a bowl for her keys, a charger for her cell phone, and a spot to drop her purse.

"Let me just see if I can get a hit." Her fingers danced across the keyboard of her laptop. She logged into the system and entered her search criteria. "Might take a minute for that to come back."

Her phone was in her handbag, so she walked across the room and grabbed it. On her return, she noticed that Coby had taken off his boots. A quick glance at the backdoor, revealed that he'd lined them up next to the door. *Miss Penny*, she thought. The family housekeeper and nanny had raised all the McGannons as her own after they'd lost their mothers. She was family in their eyes and treated as such. Laney had observed their bond many times while on the ranch and admired the respect everyone had for Miss Penny.

She also knew that Clive McGannon, Coby's uncle, had raised him. The man had done a fine job of bringing up the whole clan when Donny McGannon, Coby's father, had ditched town after cashing out his inheritance—an inheritance that was at the center of the attempted murder investigation now. Evidence suggested Donny had been searching for ways to take more of the ranch than his brother offered on his return. In her estimation, Donny should have been happy his brother gave him any status and position on the ranch at all after what he'd done.

She took a snap of the handwritten note. "I have a guy who analyzes handwriting. He might be able to give us some insight into what kind of person we might be dealing with here."

"Any person who would do something like this has to be off his rocker." Coby rubbed his eyes. He looked at her and a dozen butterflies released in her chest. "I realize that's not exactly a true statement."

"We just don't know yet. Is he calculating? Are we dealing with a *she*? Or a group? Organized crime could be involved."

Her remarks got his attention. "I just assumed we were dealing with a male. The handwriting seems masculine, plus the fact someone had to be strong enough to abduct a mother and baby gave me the impression a guy had to be involved. But I could be wrong."

"All we have to go on right now is the note and the cell phone," she surmised.

"Which isn't much. I can see if there's a number to text now that you've dusted the phone for prints," he offered.

She nodded, checking the database to see where she was in the search. Still calculating. "How about a cup of coffee while we wait?"

"I'd love one." There was a lot of enthusiasm in those words.

"How about Diesel?"

"He doesn't drink coffee." Coby shot her a look.

"Funny, wise guy. I meant water. Can I put a bowl out for him?"

"He would appreciate it. You might want to put a towel down, though." He looked around, examining her place.

Yes, she was a neat freak. And a shudder ran down her back at the thought of Diesel's slobber all over her cabinets if he decided to shake his head after taking a drink. But it could be cleaned up later and he needed to stay hydrated.

She put on a pod in the coffee machine and then grabbed a casserole dish for water. She put a dishtowel underneath to catch as much of the overflow as possible.

"How do you take yours?" she asked.

"Black is fine."

He cocked a brow when she made hers the same. Hey, she liked strong coffee. It helped her think and she was used to taking whatever she could get. Convenience store coffee. Coffee shop coffee. People offered her coffee when she came inside their homes to interview families. As long as it was hot, she was good to go.

Diesel moseyed over to the bowl she'd placed on the other side of the door, opposite Coby's boots. She opened a can of kitten food and mashed it up in a small glass bowl and set it outside.

"You don't have a cat," Coby said to her when she returned to the table.

"No."

"So what's with the food?"

"There's a feral tabby that comes around. She's young and I haven't seen siblings or a mother. I've been putting out tuna but decided to get her something with vitamins." She shrugged. "It's why I stopped off at the feed store today. That, and to get a few supplies to put out on the back porch for her if she decides to come in."

He didn't immediately speak. In fact, his thick lips formed a thin line as he seemed to be holding back what he really wanted to say.

"What?"

He shrugged. "That's unexpected coming from you."

"Why 'coming from me'?"

"You just don't strike me as an animal person." Whatever that meant.

"I can't in good conscience let the little thing starve," she said a little too quickly, and a whole lot defensively.

"I didn't mean—"

"What? That I don't have a soul? Or that I'm the kind of

person who would stand by and let a kitten starve when I could do something about it because I don't like animals?" Frustration seethed.

"You caught me off guard," he said by way of explanation. "Most people don't surprise me anymore. That's all. But you should know that I have a lot of respect for what you're doing."

The sincerity in his words caused more of that inappropriate attraction to stir.

The cell on the table vibrated, interrupting the moment. The perp.

3

The meadow.
Bring $.
Your grl will be returned.

Those three texts, back-to-back, were the equivalent of an espresso shot. The urge to respond with a promise he'd do anything required in order to save a child became a physical ache. The child didn't have to be his for him to want to save her. In fact, he had serious doubts she could belong to him, although not impossible. And yet, that didn't stop his protective instincts from kicking into high gear when anything or anyone weaker than him was in trouble.

On the other hand, he also realized this could be a bluff. The whole thing could be a charade derived for financial gain. It was common knowledge his family had more money than any one of them could spend in a lifetime. While he fully believed most folks were good-hearted, he'd seen greed play out more times than he wanted to. Jerk-offs and criminals were in no short supply. Ranching families stuck together and came to each other's aid. It was how they survived all kinds of conditions, be it mother nature or manmade. Make a wrong move and the consequences could be dire. Being part of a community saved their butts time and time again. His decision to include Laney was looking better and better.

"What's my next step?" he asked, suspecting it wouldn't have anything to do with a bank run.

She studied her screen for a long moment with her index finger to her lips—lips he didn't want to notice were full and cherry red.

"You need to find out who they have and then we'll ask for proof of life," she said after a thoughtful pause.

He picked up the cell and typed in a message. *I need names first. Girl and mother.*

Before hitting send, he tilted the screen for Laney to approve the text. She nodded and he could already see tension lines forming around her eyes and mouth. Seeing her stress levels increase with the move caused his stomach lining to braid.

He sent the message.

The three dots appeared, indicating a response was being typed. The fast response could be a good thing. He would get at least one lifeboat as he navigated shark infested waters. On the other hand, the kidnapper could realize they'd targeted the wrong person and...

Then what?

Kill the mother and child? Start over with someone else?

The fact that a mother and child hadn't been reported missing yet said there was no partner or spouse involved. Wouldn't a spouse know if his wife and child had been abducted?

There could be reasons someone would be in the dark. For one, the spouse could travel. For another, he could be at work. This could have gone down in a matter of hours.

The dots disappeared but no message came. Coby's chest squeezed as he looked at Laney, who shook her head as if to say *Don't panic yet.*

He understood that on some level even if his pulse kicked into high gear at the thought he might have made his first mistake. A deadly one? If he was the one in danger, *possible* danger, he corrected, there'd be no big deal. He knew exactly how to handle himself and was confident in his abilities to keep himself alive.

Not knowing who could be in danger was the worst feeling. Not knowing if he would make the right moves was torture. And not knowing if he could do a damn thing to make it better would haunt him.

Someone, if not him, had a daughter. One who very much deserved to stay alive.

Coby never really thought much about having children. His own father was so messed up that Coby figured it might be best not to pass those genes along into the gene pool. The world didn't need another Donny McGannon.

"Here we go," Laney said, sitting up a little straighter.

There were three dots on the screen again.

Arial.

"The name doesn't ring any bells," he admitted.

"She might go by the nickname Ari," Laney offered.

He drew a blank. "No."

"It might have been a passing fling." She studied the rim of her coffee cup like it held the answers to unlock the universe.

"This would have been a while back, and I may have been with a number of women, but I'm not the kind of person who forgets the names of the women he sleeps with." There was defensiveness in his tone he wished he could reel back in. He wasn't normally one to give away his emotions and she seemed surprised too.

"Could be the child's name," she offered. Her fingers got busy, dancing across the keyboard. She tapped her finger on the table as she waited for results. "I'm not getting any hits on similar cases to this one."

She drummed her fingers again. Then went to work on the keyboard. Shook her head a few seconds later when there wasn't much to work with.

He sent back three question marks.

Brth name. Adamson.

"He has a habit of dropping the *i* in words," Coby noted.

"Ask for proof of life," she said before going back to typing.

"If I say it like that, they'll know I'm working with a private entity or law enforcement." He smacked his palm against the table. Then he got an idea. He picked up the cell again.

How do I know they are still alive?

Because I'm tellng you!!!

Coby knew he was going to have to push back on this one. He could only pray the move wouldn't backfire because this whole situation could go south in a heartbeat. They wanted money in exchange for life. They'd kidnapped a mother and child, if they could be believed. They wouldn't want to walk out of this empty handed any more than Coby would.

No proof. No money. Period.

Coby exhaled. There wasn't much he'd come across in his years on the ranch and tracking poachers that rattled him. Until now.

"You did the right thing," Laney reassured. "Right now, we don't know what we're dealing with. This could be a hoax. An attempt to extort money. There might not be any Arial Adamson or child. I'm searching for the name right now."

"Part of me is saying this is a dangerous way to find out," he admitted, wiping the small beads of sweat that had formed on his forehead.

"Understandable."

"What's our next move?" he asked.

"You're not going to like this answer." She flashed those eyes at him. "Wait."

"You're right about that." He pushed up to standing and took a lap around her kitchen. He flexed and released his fingers a couple of times trying to work off the tension.

Could he trust Laney Justice's advice? Could he trust her opinion? Could he trust her reassurance?

Did he really have a choice?

THEY HAD A NAME. That gave them something to go on at least. Laney typed the name in a search engine along with the word, Texas. Got a few results. Not much to go on.

"This is like finding a needle in a haystack," she admitted out of frustration.

"How long do we wait?" His physical presence, and what a presence that was, oozed impatience.

"Until we hear back."

He issued a sharp sigh.

"I know that's not the answer you wanted to hear and I don't want it to be true either. If you make a move before they do, they'll know you're eager. They'll use it as a weakness."

"So, I'm involved in a game of chicken with someone I

don't know, to save a woman and child I've never met." He stabbed his fingers through his hair. "Great."

"Alleged woman and child at this point. We don't have proof they exist."

"What if some guy out there doesn't realize his family has been kidnapped? What if he would have made all the right moves?" Another sharp sigh. Diesel got up and started pacing with Coby.

"We can only deal in facts. That's all we have to go on."

"What's the likelihood this person will give me what I want?" he asked, stopping to lock gazes with her like he was trying to evaluate whether or not he trusted her responses. She was very aware of the concern he had, concern that others might not have had. His compassion was one in a long list of admirable traits.

"I don't have an answer for you, Coby. I've never been in a ransom situation before and if I was the one running this ship, we'd be calling in the FBI pronto." She shrugged when he looked displeased with the answer. "That being said, I do have a lot of experience in law enforcement and dealing with perps. I've had training to prepare me for most any situation that could come up." To be fair, most of her recent training had more to do with active shooter drills. Until recently, Cattle Cove had been a quiet little town. A wave of crime had descended on the town and she had no plans to give up or give in until she put a stop to it.

He stared out the window for a long moment. Then, issued a sharp breath before saying, "I have an overnight bag in my Jeep. Mind if I use your shower while we wait?"

"No. Go right ahead." She must have shot him a look without realizing it.

"What?"

"You keep an overnight bag in your Jeep?" she asked.

"I never know when I'm going to get called out to track poachers on a moment's notice. I keep the bag packed so I'll be ready. Everyone does at the ranch," he said like it should be public knowledge.

"Fair enough." It was logical.

He took off and she forced her gaze away from his strong back. Underneath his cotton shirt she could see his muscles cord and stretch with his movements. He had the kind of athletic grace usually reserved for elite athletes. And was causing havoc with her pulse.

She was only noticing out of habit, a job hazard, she told herself, and not because she couldn't take her eyes off Coby McGannon. Besides, he wasn't going to like her very much once she released his father.

Which, by the way, she needed to check her e-mail to see if the papers came through. They did. She needed to send word to release Donny McGannon. The urge to give Coby a heads up as to what was about to happen struck.

He slipped back in through the backdoor, quiet as a church mouse. It was Diesel who gave the pair away. His nails clicked on her tile flooring.

"Guest room is that way." She motioned toward the hallway on the opposite side of the living room.

"I won't be long." He moved past her with a backpack slung over his shoulder.

If she was going to tell him, now would be the perfect time. But, hey, she was just doing her job and she couldn't let his presence in her house throw her off track. Besides, he'd find out once his father was back at the ranch. And, honestly, he had enough on his plate with the current situation.

She sent the text to her deputy, who was on duty at the jail, and then forwarded the e-mail. She'd done this exact same routine dozens of times in the past when a prisoner was cleared for release. So, why did today feel like a betrayal?

An attraction was one thing. It had no place on the job.

Rather than analyze her actions, she did a little more digging into the name Arial. She entered several variations, Aria, Ari, Ria. The perp said this was her birth name. Laney's first thought was witness protection. But that didn't make sense.

She needed to come at this from another angle because the current one was getting her nowhere.

The perp had targeted the McGannons. It was well known they had money in spades. Specifically, Coby had been targeted. She needed to get a list of names of known associates. She needed to interview him about any disagreements he'd been in recently or if the ranch had any new hires. She knew ranch foreman meticulously vetted employees and Travis and Lawrence had been around for a long time. Was there anyone new?

As awkward as this felt, Laney also needed to get a list of all the women Coby had dated or, maybe more accurately, had rejected in the past two years. Her face felt flush thinking about asking him about his love life. It was probably too hot in her house. She needed to crank on the A/C. Then, she remembered it was chilly outside and getting cooler, not the other way around.

When Coby came walking down her hallways in a fresh pair of jeans and no shirt, towel drying his hair, that same heat crawled up her neck as her throat dried up.

Laney had spent the last three years trying to prove she was more than capable of being the first female sheriff in the county. Plus, she was still trying to gain back the trust of folks in Cattle Cove after the mess the former sheriff, Sheriff

Skinner, had left. He'd left behind a scandal involving him and the former mayor in a cover-up.

If that wasn't enough to deal with, she was in the middle of an investigation to determine who, if anyone, tried to murder Clive McGannon.

The look on Coby's face said he already knew what she'd done.

"Were you planning to let me in on the news my father was just released?" The wall between them doubled.

"I don't owe you an explanation for doing my job." Those words felt like a fraud as she heard them come out of her mouth.

"No. You don't owe me anything. Common courtesy is something else, something I expected." He had a right to be frustrated when he put it like that, and she felt like a jerk.

She clasped her hands together and placed them on top of the table. "It was a lapse in judgment on my part. It also literally just happened five minutes ago and I would have brought it up at some point before you left."

"At some point?" The disbelief in his tone was a slap in the face. He shook his head and she could sense all the walls coming up between them. As long as it put a little distance between them, she could live with it. The minute it hindered their investigation, she would need to figure out a way to break through.

For now, she was determined to put the focus back where it belonged on the case.

"I'm going to need a list of all the women you've dated or had sex with for the past two years," she said as calmly as she could despite her racing heart. She'd asked similar questions in investigations and this time was no different. A little embarrassing for the person in the opposite chair but nothing that couldn't be mitigated. "And also a list of any women who were interested in you, that you didn't pursue something with."

"You want me to start rattling off names right this second?" The words came out like a dare.

She shook her head.

And then, getting up, she walked past him in order to grab a pen and notebook from her purse. She reclaimed her seat, set the pen and notepad down on the table, and used two fingers to push it across the table to where he stood.

"Whenever you're ready," she said, slipping into cop mode. Laney was getting so used to distancing herself from her feelings to get through the day in her line of work it was becoming habit. Only time would tell if it was a good habit to develop or not. Right now, with Coby, the shine had worn off her superpower.

4

A little girl.

Coby's chest squeezed thinking about a daughter. There was no way he had fathered a child. Still not possible in his mind. But on the remote possibility he had, he'd never given much thought to what sex he'd want the baby to be. The thought of having a family couldn't be the furthest thing from his mind. Mostly because he was done with dating for now, and he'd had his fill of complicated relationships. So much about his father's situation was still up in the air. Plus, he was hardly alone. He had his brothers, cousins and their new relationships. He had Diesel.

So, why did his heart melt at the almost nonexistent possibility he had a daughter?

Coby finished drying his hair and then walked into the dining area. He took a seat across from Laney. Her nose was buried in her laptop and she barely looked up.

The empty page, however, stared back at him. Covering the last three months was easy. There'd been exactly zero dates since this whole ordeal began with his Uncle Clive.

He'd been too worried about the possibility of losing the man who'd raised him to think about spending a weekend in Austin to meet people. That was generally how dating went for someone who spent most of his time on the land working a six day a week job. Most Sundays were spent relaxing after a tough week unless it was calving season.

Call him old, but he was beginning to prefer a cold beer on a Saturday night with a game on in the background to forcing conversation with someone he barely knew. He liked pretty much all sports so it didn't matter which one was on. Although he couldn't be sure when he'd become one of those people who liked to tinker around in his home and be in bed at a decent hour. It wasn't all that long ago when he would have been the first one behind the wheel to make the drive to Austin, where there was a variety of women to choose from. He and one of his brothers or cousins would split the cost of a room. They would stand in line for an hour to eat at whatever place was popular the next day along with dozens of University of Texas at Austin coeds. After a good meal, usually involving some form of a taco, they would head home.

Austin was the perfect place to meet new people. No one knew who they were there. It was a great place to blend in and meet new people without all the baggage that came with being a McGannon. Don't get him wrong, he loved his last name and it was more of a blessing than a curse. Still, dating could be complicated and they had to be careful. One of his cousins used to routinely drop the first two letters of their last name until he got to know someone well enough to reveal the rest. It backfired at one point.

Now, none of that mattered. When this whole ordeal was finally behind them and normal life resumed, there was no one left to buddy around with in Austin. The end of an era.

It struck Coby that he was the last single McGannon left in Cattle Cove. If Laney had to ask about his love life in the future, he hoped to have a few more names to write down. The past few months netted zero. Before that, had been summer. He had to have a couple of names there.

None came to mind.

Really?

He tapped the pen on the pad of paper.

"Too many to remember?" Laney asked without making eye contact.

"Not exactly." Before summer had been calving season and seven day work weeks. He distinctly remembered dating someone for New Year's. He'd gone to that party with her at her friend's house. Elaine Bennett. He started to jot down the name but decided against it. Technically, the party had been a dud and so had the date. He'd slept on her couch, and nothing romantic happened.

Before that had been the holidays, so no one there. Last fall. Janet Hampton. They'd dated for several weeks and he definitely remembered having sex with her. He wrote down the name. Had it really been a year?

That was definitely not normal. Then again, this hadn't exactly been a normal year. Normal was a pipedream. Before Janet, there'd been a three-month long celibate relationship with Alice Gainer.

He tapped the pen. No need to write her name down.

Before Alice...

Seeing his sex life, or lack thereof, from the last couple of years reminded him just how little he'd been getting away from the ranch. He'd met plenty of women during weekend trips more than a year ago but none had held his interest long enough for a second date or casual but amazing sex. Looking at his abysmal dating record for the past year had him wanting to go out and date the next attractive person he saw just to prove to himself that he hadn't lost his touch. He almost laughed out loud at where his mind had gone with this. He'd dated plenty in the past, just not the past year. And he was okay with it.

"I'm afraid work has been keeping me busier than I realized the past year. There's only one possibility. Janet." He searched Laney's face for signs of surprise.

She was a good investigator because it was hard to read her. And it was immature as all get out that part of him wanted to add a few names to the list just to impress her. As a grown man, he didn't need a long list of conquests to prove anything and he'd never looked at women in that manner anyway.

"Then our job will be a lot easier. Do you want to call to check on her or should I?" She looked up and smiled. There was no judgment, just warmth.

"I'll do it." He grabbed his cell, hoping he'd hung onto the number. "I've dated around more than Janet but she's the only possibility for a child." He performed a mental calculation. "The baby couldn't be more than three months old and I'm ninety-nine-point-nine percent certain there's not a snowball's chance in..."

He stopped himself right there. She got the drift. No need to spell it out further.

Janet's number was still locked in his phone, so he made the call. She picked up on the first ring.

"Haven't heard from you in a long time, Coby McGannon. How have you been?" She had one of those deep whiskey-sounding voices, like a young Hollywood actress he could never remember the name of. She starred in a movie about a ghost what seemed like forever ago. In fact, that might have been the name of the movie if memory served.

"Good. Busy working, as usual." He avoided making eye contact with Laney. It seemed wrong to be on the phone with his ex while in the same room with Laney for reasons he couldn't explain. "Is everything okay with you?"

"Last time I checked, it was. Why? Do you want to make the drive to come see me in person?" She was beautiful. The kind of beauty that immediately caught the eye. Dark hair. Dark eyes. Curves. As memory served, she'd been too caught up in whatever the latest craze was to keep his interest. She cared about going to a first-run movie and shopping every weekend. Sex between them hadn't been a problem but the conversation left too much to be desired after.

"Nah. I thought I heard something. Must not have been you. Anyway, I was just calling to make sure you were good." Awkward didn't begin to describe his exit from this conversation. He was genuinely relieved that she was all right. Plus, he'd just crossed off the only fatherhood option off his list.

"Well, okay then. You call if you change your mind about coming over," she said.

"Baby...who are you on the phone with?" a male voice called out.

"No one you know. It's my cousin," she said in a hushed tone.

Coby almost laughed out loud. Looked like his judgment had been spot on with her. It was time to move on.

He ended the call and looked up at Laney, who was studying her computer screen. "It's safe to cross her name off the list."

~

LANEY WAS SHOCKED.

She was still trying to decide what she expected. A long list of names? Dozens of women in the background?

Why? She barely knew Coby, and yet she'd made unfair judgments about him already. And why had she done that? Because he was drop-dead gorgeous. The man could probably have any woman he wanted.

Maybe that was the point. Maybe he'd been there, done that, so to speak and had grown tired of meaningless interactions.

Or, maybe the guy had morals and honor and didn't use his last name to seduce women, an annoying voice in the back of her head pointed out. It was her practical side breaking through her emotions. She had been pretty unfair lumping him into a category of men most would consider jerks. And she would apologize for it if it wouldn't mean exposing her not-so-honorable thoughts about him.

As it was, he didn't know where her mind had gone. It was probably for the best she kept that part to herself. And when it came to Coby, she wouldn't mindlessly lump him into another category because of his looks or her preconceived notions about men who looked like him.

Being in law enforcement and good at her job, people didn't usually surprise Laney. Coby was a refreshing change of pace and nothing like his real father. Speaking of which, she owed Coby an apology.

"I'm sorry for earlier, by the way," she conceded.

His dark brows knitted together.

"Not telling you about your father before sending the text for his release."

"You don't owe me an explanation for doing your job." His voice was stiff. He had every reason to cold-shoulder her. She made a promise to herself to do better. She'd gotten a little too good at keeping everyone at arm's length. She could do her job effectively and professionally while showing common courtesy to those who deserved it.

"I made a judgment call. I was wrong. I'll give you a heads-up next time."

"Let's hope there isn't one," he shot back.

She'd tried to chip away at some of the ice between them. That was all she could do. Except that gaining his trust was important to the case. That was the main reason she cared and not because of any personal feelings she might have toward him.

The cell on the table buzzed.

For a second, they both just stared at it like it was a bomb about to detonate. Coby flinched ever so slightly before seeming to regain his calm demeanor. Then, he picked up the phone and checked the message.

"It's a picture of a baby all right." His teddy bear brown eyes squinted. "And that's today's date on the newspaper."

"We can't rule out the possibility the picture has been manipulated," she said as he tilted the screen toward her. "May I?"

He handed over the cell phone and then moved around the table to sit beside her. Their outer thighs grazed and a jolt of electricity rocked her body from the point of contact. She ignored it as she studied the photograph.

"This is a newborn. She can't be more than a few weeks old. Maybe a month," she informed. "Based on your time-line and conversation with your ex, the mother of this child would have gotten pregnant around New Year's."

"Then there's no way she's mine." Those words shouldn't have had an effect on Laney one way or the other. It surprised her how much they did. Whether or not Coby had fathered a child or not was none of her concern on a social level. Normally, she could compartmentalize her feelings and distance herself from any personal feelings while working on a case. It was important to be able to do her job efficiently and to keep her sane. The ability to distance herself from her emotions was a good quality, and one she couldn't afford to lose no matter how devastatingly handsome Coby was. Or how much she was drawn to him. To be fair, he had the whole sexy cowboy bit down pat without even trying. But it was so much more than physical appearance that had her looking at him twice. His eyes—windows to the soul as everyone said—had a depth like she'd never seen before. He'd displayed nothing but honor and honesty. Then, there was the fact he was more concerned about strangers than his own safety.

"The question is, why would someone target you for the money if it had nothing to do with you?" She needed to keep her thoughts on track. An attraction wasn't just a distraction, it was reckless.

"I'm drawing a blank," he admitted.

"The mother could have panicked after she and her baby were abducted. She might have ruled out the baby's father as being helpful." A mother trying to protect her child would do almost anything.

"But what if I'd thrown the note and cell phone away, refusing to help?"

Laney tapped her finger on the table. "That's a really good point actually. This person might have some inside knowledge of you and your family. She might know that you're a decent person and would move heaven and earth to help a stranger in trouble."

"Given my family's financial position, she wouldn't be the first person to try to involve one of us for money's sake."

A person would be hard-pressed to find Laney feeling sorry for someone whose biggest problem was how much money their family had. But, in this case, she actually had sympathy for Coby for just that reason.

It was easy to think having more money would solve most of life's problems. She'd grown up in a loving family who definitely couldn't have been categorized as rich. Her parents had fought about money and, for a while, she thought having more of it would make everything all right. Maybe even save her parents' unhappy marriage.

But then she'd grown up and realized life was more complicated. A few extra zeroes in the bank account wouldn't have caused her parents to get along any better than they did. They'd stayed together and by all accounts were a 'nice' family. People didn't see the other side. The one where she'd stayed up late at night unable to sleep while her parents fought over basically everything. Money had only been one hot topic. So was pretty much anything to do with the way the girls were being brought up. Then, there were the constant comparisons. Laney had been the smart one. Her sister had been the beautiful one. Oh, and her personal favorite of being forced to choose between their parents.

Funny how those labels from childhood stuck with a person long after they'd outgrown them in every possible way, physically and emotionally.

"It's possible," she circled back to the conversation after getting lost in her head for a few moments.

Coby was in his own head too. He'd taken the cell from her hand and was studying it intensely. Looking for any signs of a family resemblance?

"My first thought when I got the ransom note was this had to be a joke. My second was that it had to be a mistake. Someone had put the note on the wrong vehicle. This town has more Jeeps than a dealership." It was an exaggeration but she got the point. "But what if this baby belongs to one of my brothers or cousins?"

"I can send out an e-mail, asking if any of your brothers has ever met anyone by the name of Arial. I don't have to give a reason. They'll most likely assume this has to do with your father's case," she offered.

"They won't be any the wiser if the e-mail comes from you. If someone in the family did father the child, he clearly was never told. We share everything and this would be huge news considering she would be the second grandchild in the family." He tapped the screen. "The date looks good, though. This pic is from today."

"You should probably respond to them, asking for their demands." The thought was sobering.

I believe you. How much $?

Laney didn't realize she'd been holding her breath until the next message came through.

250k for the grl

"Ask about the mother," Laney urged.

2-for-1?

The dots appeared on the screen, indicating the other party was typing a response. The message came through a few seconds later.

No.

5

"Can you figure out where this call is coming from?" Coby asked Laney, figuring the signal had to ping off cell towers somewhere that could be traced. He wasn't the most technical person. Or into devices or machines. Ask him his preference and he'd say that he would take a horse over a truck any day. The answer was a no brainer.

"I don't have the resources or the authority to trace a call on an investigation I'm technically not on."

"Looks like we're going to the meadow then." A cold chill raced down his spine thinking about going back to the spot where two pre-teens were murdered years ago. The cover-up that was only recently dispelled, thanks in no small part to Laney herself, had been all over the news. In fact, when Ensley, the older sister of one of the teens, came back to Cattle Cove to prove her younger brother was murdered, his cousin Levi got involved. He and Ensley fell in love in the process of finding justice.

The thought of the baby in the picture being taken out to the woods to that very place stirred up red-hot anger. The infant had clearly been crying and she had the sweetest pout. Seeing her upset literally made his heart ache. She looked good otherwise, healthy. So, that had to be a good sign she was being taken care of. He couldn't imagine a mother who would use her child to extort money out of someone but he couldn't ignore the possibility either. A desperate mother might do desperate things in order to provide for her child. Was there anyone he'd come across in the past year who was pregnant?

Wasn't there someone at a party on the lake who threw up more than once and drank water all night instead of alcohol? A friend of his ex-girlfriend's?

It was quite a leap to go from throwing up at a party to being pregnant. Calving season was always a blur and that started in February. He'd gone down to the lake a couple of times during January.

Or was she there then? It was possible he was mixing up his timeline. Memories had a way of jumbling from February to the time to go to the stockyard in the summer. It was a blur of tagging and logging and making sure everyone was healthy. There was a lot of weighing and fourteen hour days.

Coby didn't mind the long hours. He didn't mind the work. It was a satisfying part of the job. But he couldn't exactly expect himself to remember much else when he was constantly going on black coffee and three to four hours of sleep.

"What's the plan?" He knew Laney had one or was cooking one up at the very least.

"Obviously, they have to think you're going alone," she said. "If memory serves, cell service is spotty there."

The list of things that could go wrong at a drop spot was long. Add in the fact there would be little to no cell service, and he was asking for trouble. He could encounter any number of things in the meadow. It could be a trap to get him out somewhere alone where he could be kidnapped and held for ransom, which would be ironic and also kind of brilliant if anyone asked him.

Normally, he spent his time on the ranch, which had endless security and wasn't easily accessible. He ventured off the property now and again. Less since the whole incident with his uncle started.

So, it was possible that someone knew the best way to lure him off the property was with a woman and baby in distress. No McGannon would turn away from a mother and child in danger. Then, they gave him instructions to come out to a meadow, alone, with a boatload of cash. Didn't they realize his bank would be suspicious of a withdrawal of that size? There would be questions and it would take a minute to get the cash together. Even after all that was done, where did that leave him? As a sitting duck.

Great plan. No thanks.

"I need to let them know it will take time to get the money together," he said. "That should give us a little time to figure out a plan."

"They'll push for the money ASAP," she noted, tapping her toe on the tile flooring. He figured as much.

"They'll get it when I can arrange it." He picked up the cell.

I need two days.

The response was almost instant. *No.*

Then, when?

Another response came. *24 hrs*

That's too soon.

There were no dots, no response. Only the image of a

ticking clock. Coby glanced at the time. It read two-forty-five. He needed to keep the time in mind.

"Come look at this," Laney suggested.

He walked over and took a seat next to her. Her unique scent, all flowers and fresh spring mornings, overtook his senses as he breathed. Under normal circumstances, he would enjoy the way his throat dried up and stomach clenched when he was anywhere near her.

This was the woman who had been making a case against his father for attempted murder. Keeping that thought at the forefront of his mind would be the smart thing to do. It would force him to keep a safe distance when his fingers itched to get lost in that thick hair of hers.

An image, nothing more than a flash really, popped into his thoughts. It was him and Laney, naked, together, the sheets all around them in a twist. Smiling. Still gasping for air. Satisfied beyond any expectations he could have had.

Guilt washed over him. He shouldn't be having sexy, naked thoughts about the sheriff. He avoided meeting her eyes even though he could feel her gaze on him. Tabling that thought was the best thing he could do as he refocused on the screen.

"We can get a good aerial view here and map out our plans." She'd pulled up a map from a popular search engine.

"I need to make a quick call before we get too far into this." Coby fished his cell from his pocket. He pulled up Jack's name and made the call, turning away from Laney and the judgment he was certain to face. "I need to make a quarter of a million dollars show up tomorrow morning, first thing."

"Done. Anything else?" Jack wasn't one to mince words. He was 'the guy' Coby and any of his brothers called if they needed something done off the books. It rarely came up but sure was handy. There were no questions asked and, this way, he wouldn't have to go through the hassle of the bank.

"See you at the feed store at nine o'clock sharp," Coby said.

"Yes, sir."

When he turned back, the shock on Laney's face was a gut punch.

"I hope that was a legal transaction," she said with a grimace.

"It was. He's a person we call when we need something and want to stay under the radar. Most of the time, we're using him to make a purchase like a lake house or beach property. Sometimes it's a horse. If a seller knows a McGannon is making the offer, the price suddenly doubles overnight." He shouldn't be as offended as he was by the look or the questions. Being a McGannon, he forgot how making that kind of money show up no questions asked might look to an outsider.

"Oh." She glanced at him with an apologetic look.

"It's okay. Don't even worry about it." He was more disappointed than he wanted to let on that she would think he could be involved in something illegal. Then again, his father had had a gambling addiction that had been kept out of the public eye for years. Those close to the family knew but only the inner circle. McGannons kept each other's secrets.

"I'm sorry. I had preconceived notions about your family that have been blasted through while investigating..." she paused and her gaze unfocused like she was looking inside herself for the answer, "the case."

"And now?"

She exhaled slowly and it was like a balloon deflating.

"I've learned how wrong I've been. Getting to know your brothers and cousins through the investigation has proved time and time again that your family holds high moral ground. It's easy to look at your family from the outside and think money is the reason you guys are so close-knit and, seemingly, happy. But you have challenges just like the rest of us. You have disappointments just like the rest of us. Maybe more because you guys each suffered loss at such a young age." She flashed her eyes at him. "I apologize for the intrusive remark. I couldn't be sorrier for your loss."

He compressed his lips, thinking he needed to hold his tongue. She was on track about everything but his family being close. They used to be. But the chasm between his brothers and their cousins seemed so wide that it wasn't funny. And he had no idea how to get back to the place where they were comfortable with each other again. So, he nodded, which seemed to give her permission to keep going.

"The way everyone accepted Kurt and his daughter was truly remarkable." She put a hand up to stop him from disagreeing. "I do realize there was a bumpy start to the relationship, and a lot of that was on Kurt. He came in prickly, wanting nothing to do with the family or the ranch."

"Not exactly true. He wanted family for his daughter. He just wasn't sure if he'd found it or if we'd accept her," he pointed out.

"But you did. Every last one of you welcomed her."

"My last name is a blessing and a curse. The blessing is that we stick together." He let that thought percolate when he considered what his uncle had done for his father. Uncle Clive was the best example of family sticking together. He was defending his brother, posting bail even, when no one could prove their father didn't try to kill the man. Was that blind loyalty? Wishful thinking? Or was Uncle Clive *that* certain about his only brother?

The move shocked everyone but maybe it shouldn't have. Coby's personal cell started blowing up. He picked it up and checked the screen. There were multiple messages from his brothers and cousins.

From the gist of the texts, it looked like Uncle Clive wanted a family meeting to explain why he'd invited his brother back into the main house.

"Everything all right over there?" Laney's brow was hiked up.

"That depends on who you ask," he said, staring at his phone. Based on the texts, no one was thrilled with the move.

THE BOND between McGannon brothers and cousins ran thick. Even Laney had witnessed the stress cracks forming despite the closeness. She wanted to pick Coby's brain about his family while she had access to him. Another case—this case—was taking priority and it was still too early to ascertain whether or not she was dealing with amateurs or pros.

There were people who did this for a living. They were skilled and it would be impossible to trick them.

"I have drones we could use tomorrow to keep watch on the area. We could set them up hours beforehand. There would be risks," she said to Coby, steering her thoughts back on track.

"The perp might get there before us and have drones or other security devices set up. Almost anything can be ordered off the internet now," he admitted. "It wouldn't be difficult to set up. Plus, we have no idea how many people we're looking at."

"There could be one or two, or this could be part of a bigger crime ring," she agreed.

"What are the chances this person is after me specifically? That they want to isolate me?"

"It can't be ruled out," she said. "Which is one of many reasons that I think it's a good idea to involve the feds. You didn't recognize the little girl in the text."

He shook his head and she hoped she was getting through to him.

"And you don't know who they have. We can't find a name via a search engine. This person is likely someone from your past or someone who knows you."

"What do you make of them stating Arial was her birth name?" This close, she didn't want to breathe in his spicy male scent even though that's exactly what happened. His clean masculine scent washed over her and through her. Fighting against it was like trying to fight a riptide. She gave herself a mental slap to refocus. "Just that she went by a nickname."

"Why not go ahead and tell me who she is? Why make me guess?"

"This person is toying with us, with you. It could mean we are dealing with someone with a high IQ who is a couple of steps ahead of the game at all times. And that's exactly what this could be to them. A game. They might be trying to rattle your cage or pull attention away from your dad's case." The McGannon case had returned to being her main focus. "On the other hand, we could be dealing with someone who is desperate for money. They might have overheard someone use your name and then snatched them, figuring they could turn a quick profit. The amount of money requested is a drop in the bucket for someone like you."

He shot her a look.

"You might not view it that way but others do. He might think the request is so small for you that you'll hand it over just to make him go away," she defended.

"That's a lot of money. I don't care who you are," he said low and under his breath.

"I'm not trying to offend you. I'm just looking at this from the perp's perspective and trying to see all the possible angles." She paused, unsure if she should admit this or not. On balance, she figured it couldn't hurt. "For what it's worth, you and your family are some of the most down-to-earth people I've ever met, especially as a family who is pretty damn well off."

The compliment seemed to embarrass him.

"We're just people like everyone else," he said.

Laney could refute that on so many levels. Most people weren't as honorable as the McGannons. Granted, Donny McGannon was the exception to the rule. However, didn't all families have that one bad egg?

When it came to everyone else in the family, she could mount an argument that each one, and she knew this to be true, contributed financially to charities. They did it quietly and without fanfare, never expecting a pat on the back for their activities while most would have a camera crew on the ready to document every ounce of generosity.

Call it cowboy code, but McGannons were the first to offer a hand-up to anyone in need. Again, they didn't feel the need to broadcast their generosity like so many did today. It was almost as though nothing happened unless it was captured on social media these days. And there was just a huge ick factor about that. Laney had never seen the need to have a personal page anywhere other than a professional networking site. Her office kept a page but she wasn't the one responsible for making updates.

She'd been treated with nothing but kindness by each and every one of Coby's cousins and brothers, while investigating numerous cases over the past few months. Plus, no one drove a fancy car or wore expensive jewelry. If someone didn't know them any better, they'd say the McGannons were average folks.

And don't even get her started on their willingness to roll up their sleeves and pitch in for just about everything. The local church's annual pumpkin patch? Most of them showed up at some point despite never setting foot inside the building. They took shifts hauling pumpkins and setting up in the church parking lot.

Christmas? They helped cut down and haul the town's Christmas tree. They showed up for events, working behind the scenes to ensure everyone had a good time and without regard for how many hours they'd worked that day or how tired they were.

If someone asked, they'd wave them off and grab a fresh cup of coffee so they could go another couple of rounds. There were times during investigations when she wondered if any of them ever slept. She suspected they could get by on a couple hours of shuteye. They tracked down poachers on their land and turned over clean arrests.

So, she begged to differ about his family being like everyone else. They were so much better than the average person. Because of his kindness, could someone see Coby as easy pickings?

The perp had no idea who he was messing with if that was the case.

6

A host of scenarios could be likely, Coby thought as he replayed his conversation with Laney in his head. There wasn't a whole lot to go on and not a lot of time to figure out a plan before the first drop was to be made. The perp was leading with the baby. Did he think Coby would care about the mother more? Was he tired of the kid crying? Was he trying to torture the mother? It was an interesting move, to say the least.

Would any of his family know who the mystery woman was? It was possible. But that could also mean involving more people. At the very least, alerting them and causing them to have more questions. Asking those questions could get them in trouble. They would also be concerned for him and, to Laney's point, want to roll up their sleeves and help.

There had to be a way he could ask without raising any red flags. Could he approach it as a casual question without giving away the gravity of the situation?

The baby, the accusation that he was a father, reminded him just how much he knew that wasn't the path for him. There was a time when he believed he had a future and could be the kind of father Uncle Clive was. Kind. Patient. Giving. He was the most honorable person Coby had ever met.

But Uncle Clive wasn't his father. Donny McGannon was. And those genes were probably in there somewhere, latent maybe, but waiting. Like a wolf creeping up on its prey, they would emerge leaving a child helpless. Don't even get him started on the possibilities if something happened to the mother, like in his case.

He couldn't imagine having a family without a partner. In truth, he also figured she would be his moral compass should those less-than-desirable traits kick in from his father.

When he looked at Laney, he saw the kind of person he'd envisioned spending the rest of his life with. Someone who was strong-minded, intelligent, and easy to be around. Someone he wanted to come home to every night. Someone he couldn't wait to end the workday for, because he knew what was waiting at home was even better than being outside during a Texas sunset. That bar was high.

Was it an impossible standard? His brothers and cousins had joked that it was, but then look at them all now, settled down with women who'd hold them to that exact standard. And as for him? There was no way he would settle when it came to a decision that affected the rest of his life, that affected his family.

Once Donny returned, the vision of a family slowly faded. Because those were the genes inside Coby, not Uncle Clive's. That was the cancer waiting for the right conditions to multiply and destroy all the good cells. It would only be a matter of time before it succeeded in taking away everything good. Becoming a parent was about the worst thing he could do to a child, in his opinion.

On the off chance, and it was highly unlikely, the baby in the text was his, he would step up and do the right thing. That was a no brainer. But as much as part of him wished that it would be so, it was probably for the best that she wasn't.

A text came through on his phone. He picked up his phone and checked the screen. The perp. He read it to Laney. "They want the money in a paper feed store bag."

"We can make that happen. What else do they want?" she asked.

He studied the screen, waiting for more. Seconds ticked by and nothing came. Then, minutes. "I have a message for them."

Do you know who I am?

The phone had to be in their hand or at the very least near them because the perp had only just sent a message minutes ago.

After a few more silent moments, the text came through.

Coby

"Whoever this has the right person," he said to Laney. All hope this could be a case of mistaken identity shriveled and died. "He mentioned me by name."

"Now, to piece together who this Arial person could be," she said, resigned. Had she been hoping for a case of mistaken identity too? "We need to widen that list." She pointed toward the notepad. "To pretty much everyone you've dated casually, even once, in the past two years."

"Based on the age of the baby and my schedule, it's safe to focus on the timeline of a year and a half ago to two years," he said.

She nodded.

He tried to think back. This couldn't be someone he dated more than once or twice. There was a possibility it could be an acquaintance of someone he'd met. Another frustrating possibility nailed him. This could be someone he didn't know at all. It could be someone who'd fixated on him and then they really were searching for a needle in a haystack.

"I need more to go on than her birth name," he stated out loud.

"How do you plan to get that from the perp?"

"Simple. This is down to finances. He wants what I have. Other than a deep appreciation for life and motherhood, I have no reason to give the perp anything."

"What would you do? Threaten to walk away? That could end badly," she warned.

"Yes. This could too. I could do everything this jerk wants down to a T and he could still harm mother and baby. I keep going over this in my mind and coming up with the same problem. I have no leverage other than money. I don't even know who I'm dealing with but I'm done playing scared. If he wants money, he'll give a name." He probably sounded more confident in the plan than he actually was. There was no way on earth he'd do anything intentionally to put a mother and her child in harm's way. But this was ridiculous. His name had been brought up specifically. The perp knew who Coby was, and he still had no idea what he was working with on the other side.

I need her name. His finger hovered over the arrow that would send the message. There'd be no taking it back once he dipped that finger and touched the screen. He could only pray his move would pay off and not backfire.

No

Not unexpected. *Then no deal.*

Coby stared at the screen, waiting for a response. His imagination started running wild at what could be happening about now on the other end of this phone. He pushed up to standing and made a circle around the kitchen area.

He checked the phone and there was nothing. Had he angered the perp? Had he just cost the lives of two people?

His chest squeezed and acid slammed into the pit of his stomach. He made a couple more laps before checking the phone again.

Still nothing.

All the oxygen sucked out of the room and he couldn't breathe. Air. He needed air. Coby made a beeline for the backdoor. He didn't realize he'd been holding his breath until he stepped outside and into the cooler temperatures.

Jesus, what had he just done? Had he played the wrong card? Forced the perp's hand?

The picture of the newborn popped into his thoughts. An anger deeper and hotter than anything he'd ever experienced filled him at the thought of the perp touching one hair on that head of hers. Those blue eyes and her thick black hair resembled him a little bit. But, no, there was no way he'd fathered her. The news didn't stop him from caring, especially now that there was a face to the threat. She didn't have to be his for him to care what happened to her. She was *someone's* child.

If she was his child and someone had the ability to help her but didn't...he couldn't go there hypothetically about how crazy that would make him or the dark places he would go in his mind.

He tried to recall the description of the sick party goer. Did she have blue eyes? Black hair?

The back door opened and Laney appeared with Diesel by her side. She held up the cell phone, and said, "We have a name."

"SARAH HOUSER IS THE MOTHER. The little girl's name is Arial, not the mom's," Laney announced as Coby made a beeline toward her. His relief was palpable even though she could tell the news was taking a second to fully sink in.

The intensity of those eyes sent literal goosebumps through her. Any time they were in proximity to each other the air changed and heat ricocheted through her. This time was no different. If anything, more sensations were adding to the list. Ones like sensual shivers skittering across her skin.

"Sarah?" Forehead wrinkled, eyes narrowed, the name didn't seem to be ringing any bells for him.

Laney nodded, handing over the phone. "Let's search for her online and see what we come up with. We might get lucky and get a picture or a hit on social media."

At least they had something to work with now.

"And I can check to see if any Sarah Houser's have been reported missing," she added as they filed back inside. She didn't mind searching for someone Coby didn't know.

"This person might be an acquaintance of someone I've dated. There was a woman, and I'm not sure she ever told me her name, at a party I went to after New Year's. The time after is a blur with the work on the ranch but I distinctly remember going outside to stand by the lake and get some air to find a woman tossing her cookies over the deck."

"The party host might know who she is," Laney offered. "Did you get a good look at her?"

"I'd remember if I saw her again. Details are a little fuzzy for me right now," he admitted, quickly adding, "not because I was drunk or anything. I'm not big on being out of control. But I was tired and I'd driven down for the party.

The relationship with the person I had gone out with a few times was over. She surprised me with the party and I was biding my time until I could figure out a good moment to let her know I wasn't coming back."

"Was she into you?" Laney couldn't imagine a woman who wouldn't be. The man was sex on a stick, for heaven's sake. Don't even get her started on the body that went with the face—a face she wouldn't mind waking up to in the morning.

It wasn't unprofessional to think those thoughts. She was, after all, human. But it would be crossing a line to act on them. So she forced her gaze away from full, thick lips that spread over perfectly white, perfectly straight teeth.

"From what I recall, she wasn't thrilled with the breakup," he admitted. "I'd underestimated us. To me, we didn't hit it off enough to take things to the next level. She saw it another way."

"Did she threaten you in any way?" The question had to be asked.

"She said a few things she would probably regret sober. The nondrinking was on my part. She was more than happy to polish off a bottle of wine, although that was another reason I knew we'd never be a good fit. The couple of times we went out, she drank a little too much for my taste. The first time, I chalked it up to nerves."

"First dates can be stressful," she admitted, thinking she hadn't had nearly enough of those since taking the job three years ago. In fact, this case was highlighting just how little she'd dated and how little her former dates stacked up to the guy currently in the room. That needed to change. Once her workload slowed down, she would take a cue from the McGannons and head to Austin to meet people. She was young and needed companionship. The job also highlighted how lonely she'd become. Was it an excuse to close off the world? To shut herself in and not put herself out there anymore?

Possibly. She couldn't ignore the voice telling her she'd thrown herself into the job for more reasons than wanting to prove she was capable.

"Have you ever polished off a bottle of wine on a date?" His eyebrow shot up.

"I'd fall asleep if I finished off two large glasses of wine, I'm afraid. Probably doesn't make me the most fun date ever. Call me old fashioned but I like to be awake long enough to enjoy dessert."

Her comment elicited a devastating grin.

"It's good that a woman isn't afraid to eat on a date. Picking at a salad while finishing off a bottle of wine was pretty much a red flag for me."

"At least she wasn't the one driving, I hope."

"Why doesn't it surprise me a member of law enforcement had that thought? I bet it was your first thought," he said.

Not technically. Her first thought was the woman was a fool to need alcohol while on a date with Coby. Once one got past his devastating good looks, he was a normal guy. Better than normal, actually. He was a decent and caring person.

How many other people did she know who would put their own safety on the line for a mother and child they didn't know? It was a short list. Most would defer to her and her office—not that she was opposed to that approach—and call it a day. Some would follow up in a couple of days to see if everything turned out okay. But to seriously put themselves in danger? Not many.

"I can't imagine anyone needing to drink themselves

under the table while on a date with you, Coby," she piped up. Seriously. She shook her head. "What was your date's name?"

"Jackie..." he glanced at her, "I'm lost on the last name. It's been a while."

"Any chance you saved her number?" she asked.

"I always save the number," he said quickly. It shouldn't sting, considering she had no designs on him, even though it did. She couldn't even make a move if she wanted to. "In case they call again out of the blue. That way, I know who is calling."

"Actually, I'm borrowing that one. That's a really good idea."

"I've been burned in the past by deleting the numbers. Someone calls. You're expecting a follow-up call from a repair guy or doctor visit, so you answer. Bam. Now, you're stuck in an awkward conversation with someone after a relationship ended. Someone wants to give it another try despite how clear you were on that not being a possibility," he said.

She imagined he left a whole trail of heartbreak in his wake. Not because he wasn't honest with people. Not because he was a jerk. He seemed like one of the most upfront people she'd ever met.

The trail behind him would be from women who weren't ready to let go or accept the fact he'd moved on. Considering the fact he was the total package and a man like him wasn't exactly easy to come by, there had to be broken hearts.

Another reason she shouldn't let herself get too caught up in the attraction growing between them. At least she hoped it was. The electricity coursing between them couldn't be one-sided, could it? She was almost certain he felt the same despite his poker face giving away very little. And if she went down that road, the attraction thing, she was certain he would be fair with her.

And she was also certain she'd end up with a broken heart even if he felt the same attraction. There was something about Coby that warned her not to get too close. Because when he walked away—and he would—her heart would be shattered into a thousand tiny pieces.

7

C oby had a lead.

He made a beeline for his cell phone and skimmed the contact list. Since he couldn't come up with a last initial, he cross-referenced with her first name and the letter J. There were quite a few names to scroll through before he landed on hers. Jackie.

There it was. Plain as the nose on his face. A quick phone call might be able to clarify the reason Sarah Houser had tagged him as father of her child. *Here goes nothing.*

Coby tapped the name on the screen and the line started ringing.

No answer. He let it continue to ring, hoping she would pick up. It was possible that she was still mad at him over the breakup. It was even likely that she'd sworn him off. She had seemed more upset than normal considering how short their relationship—if it could be called that name—had been.

Everyone was different and everyone took the news differently. No matter how honest he was, and he was always upfront about his intentions from the start, the occasional hurt feeling seemed unavoidable. He hated it. He never set out to hurt anyone.

"Think I should leave a message?" he asked Laney when Jackie's voicemail kicked in.

"No. More mystery this way and a better chance she'll call back." Laney finished her sentence at almost the exact time Jackie's message ended. He hung up before the beep. "Most people keep their cell phones on them twenty-four-seven unless work stops them from checking it. Hopefully, she'll call back in a couple of minutes."

Coby exhaled sharply. Waiting, patience, those weren't normally problems for him. This, however, frustrated him. He second-guessed whether or not to leave the message. He'd deferred to Laney, which wasn't something he was used to doing. He respected her and her experience. She was smart and good at her job, not to mention sexy beyond anything he'd imagined he'd be thinking about the town's sheriff. He could acknowledge his attraction to her even though he couldn't act on it. But, yes, his instincts had said the same thing as she had. Wait.

He tapped his foot on the tile.

Five minutes passed with no call back. Then, ten. At the fifteen minute mark, he figured she might not call back at all.

"Jackie's house is drivable from here. We could get there by dinner time and there are plenty of places downtown that we could grab a bite to eat. A lot of places have outdoor seating and are dog friendly if we eat downtown? We might be able to catch her at home after," he suggested. Anything would be better than sitting there doing nothing. Granted, they were brainstorming the case and Laney had the map of the meadow area up. They could make progress on those fronts, which were equally important.

"If she doesn't call back in half an hour, I can call for a wellness check," she offered. The words struck like a blow. Did she think something or someone could be keeping Jackie from returning the call?

In that case, he wanted to check for himself. His name was somehow mixed up in this mess and he needed to get to the bottom of it without putting anyone else at risk.

"You don't want to check for ourselves?" The question had to be asked.

Laney leaned over the table and clasped her hands together. She rested her chin on top and he forced his gaze away from the adorable mole on the left side of her chin. "The perp could be watching her house. He might be expecting us. He might have booby traps set up or someone there on a full-time basis. At this point, I just don't know. Generally, with a case similar to this, we're talking about a straight-up opportunist. I don't yet have a feel for this perp, and I can't bring in psych experts to help for obvious reasons." She didn't say it would be breaking her word to him but that's what hung in the air and it was true.

"We do know more than we did a few hours ago," he pointed out.

"That's very true." She didn't say her experience with ransom cases was limited. They both knew it was. Crime in this area was rare until recently. Of course, they were just learning about cover-ups from the former sheriff and coroner. There could be more crimes coming to light as the cases were picked through and re-examined. Laney's office must have been flooded with anyone who ever thought they had a grievance against Skinner.

"We'll be careful," he said, referring to the home visit. "And we'll throw them off by you coming as my date."

An emotion flashed behind her eyes when he said the

last word. It wasn't something he could pinpoint and it was gone in a flash.

She breathed in slowly. "They are also expecting a cowboy. We could find a way to dress you up in something else. Maybe we can pick up a hoodie and sweatpants?"

He must have given her a look because she quickly added, "Or just a hoodie and tennis shoes."

"I have an old pair in the backseat of my Jeep," he offered.

"You and your family are the most prepared for any circumstance that life can throw at you than anyone I think I've ever met in my life," she said and there was a hint of admiration among the amusement in her voice that he didn't want to stir his heart.

"Job hazard, I'm afraid. We do pretty much have to be ready for anything man or Mother Nature can dish out. Too many times, we're called last minute to be away from home for days on end with no time to stop by the house and pack a bag. It's a rancher's life to be prepared," he said.

"I've known Boy Scouts who were less prepared than you and your family," she mused.

It made him smile. Because if she knew the thoughts he kept forcing at bay about her, she might not compare him to a Boy Scout anymore.

His thoughts were unholy and had him wanted to run a lazy finger down her curves, feel her creamy skin under his rough hands. He wanted to capture the little mole next to those cherry lips with his. And he wanted to...

Way to go, McGannon. Way to keep feelings in check.

Since he had no plans to let this runaway train go any further, he refocused on the case.

"I'll take that as a compliment, by the way," he said.

"It's intended as one." She smiled for the briefest time and those light green eyes of her lit up.

"So, we're going to check on Jackie?" It was more statement than question.

Laney stared at his phone for a long moment. "It looks like it."

"I'll get ready." He busied himself giving food and water to Diesel. The dog needed to be taken out next. While outside, Coby jogged over to where he'd stashed his Jeep two streets over, near a playground at the end of the road. He retrieved a hoodie and his tennis shoes, Diesel was by his side the entire time. He needed the exercise, so they made a couple of laps around the playground to get the heart rate up. Coby could think better when his blood was pumping.

Was there anyone else Sarah Houser could be connected to? Did Jackie and Sarah know each other? Just because they might have been at the same party doesn't mean they would know each other. They might know each other through friends of friends as was often the case at lake parties.

The fact Jackie hadn't answered was messing with his mind. His imagination took over and he envisioned her hurt or tied up, gagged.

By the time he got back to Laney's house, he'd worked up a good sweat and a great deal of concern. It was good they were going to check out her place for themselves. If she didn't want anything to do with him, fine. He wouldn't argue there after breaking up with her. She had every right not to speak to him again. He just needed to see for himself that she was okay. He wanted to know if she was connected in any way to Sarah, but that came second to Jackie being okay.

She'd always picked up by the second ring when he

called in the past. There were three critical words to that sentence, *in the past.*

He reminded himself of the fact so he wouldn't go crazy with worry. There was no telling who else Sarah Houser had brought into this mess. He had questions for her that needed answers.

Soon, he thought. Soon, he'd know if she was involved and how, or if she was in a ditch.

LANEY TOOK one look at Coby as he walked in the door, face flush from running, head down and covered by a hoodie. He looked the part of a model from a sports clothing catalogue, not a cowboy. She hoped this would be enough to cover his identity. He'd been determined to visit this Jackie person despite her reservations about doing so.

Rather than have him go off on his own, digging around where he didn't belong, she decided to go with him. Technically, she was off duty. But all this could be billed as an undercover assignment. That described it perfectly. Since she was the top law enforcement official in the county, it was her call to make whether or not to include others in her investigation.

Was she justifying her actions? Yes. Was she compartmentalizing her feelings while doing so? Yes. Was she right about being the one in charge? Also, yes.

But if this thing went south—and she had no plans to allow that to happen—it would be her butt in a sling. Technically, her job on the line. Neither appealed to her.

While Coby was out with his dog, she was able to do a little digging into Sarah Houser's life. "Sarah doesn't have a record."

"That's good." Coby stood at the kitchen sink. He'd poured himself a glass of water.

"I was able to call in a favor and get confirmation from the county hospital in Austin that a little girl by the name of Arial McGannon was born eight weeks ago." The news had shocked her but he didn't seem upset.

The soft mewling sounds of the tabby sounded next to the door. Laney hopped up and moved to the kitty. She needed to make sure the little thing was okay.

Coby cocked an eyebrow, and then followed. Diesel was right behind him.

"There you are." Laney bent down and scooped the little furball up before Diesel could hurt her. Would he, though? He was around so many animals at the ranch he was probably used to just about everything.

She picked up the kitty and held it to her chest. Coby reached over and scratched the little girl behind the ear.

"She's not feral," he said. "Someone's been taking care of her."

Laney blinked at him. "I have."

"Have you been handling her like this the whole time?" His brow went up again.

"Not at first. She's been warming up to me lately, though."

"Looks like you have yourself a pet." His smile was devastating and her heart skipped a couple of beats.

"No, I don't," she tried to argue as Diesel stuck his nose toward the tabby.

The kitty swatted at him and he didn't so much as bat an eyelash. Laney set the little girl down next to the bowl and she darted away. "Oh, no."

"She'll be back," Coby soothed.

He was right. She knew it. And yet, she needed to know

the kitty was okay.

"She's not my child. It doesn't mean that I won't do everything I can to save her life–I won't work any less hard to get her back–but I'm one hundred percent certain that she's not mine," he said with the kind of confidence that made her believe it too as he followed Laney back inside.

"I can't figure out why she would give the baby the last name McGannon," Laney said. "You had a brief interaction with her at a party. She was sick at the time. How much could she have been paying attention to who you were?"

"There have been times in the past when someone claimed one of us fathered a child, just to snag the last name," he said on a shrug. "I'm not the kind of person who thinks like they do, so it's impossible for me to figure out why they pull something like that."

"Desperation. Greed. A bunch of words come to my mind," she said.

"The dark side to having the last name McGannon."

"That must get old," she said, stalling for time in the hopes Jackie would call and they'd be spared a trip. She didn't mind the road trip in and of itself. But the thought they could be walking into a trap loomed large.

"Yeah," he admitted. "The good far outweighs the bad. But having to have my guard up when I first meet someone is a pain in the backside."

She flashed eyes at him and grinned. She knew exactly what that acronym stood for. And she couldn't agree more that it was appropriate under the circumstances.

"Although, I feel like I've been in hibernation for a long time." His admission surprised her.

"Why don't you make more of an effort to get out and date?" She couldn't imagine there wouldn't be a line of women on the ready if he snapped his fingers.

"To be honest, I feel like I'm starting to date the same person over and over again, but in a different shell," he said before finishing off the glass of water.

Boy, could she relate to the sentiment. Her last three relationships didn't even look all that different on the outside. Tall. Runner's build. Sandy-blond hair. The only difference was eye color. One had blue eyes and the other two had brown.

"Dating isn't as fun as it's cracked up to be after a certain point," he said.

She had to agree.

He glanced up and caught her eye. The air in the room changed. Unspoken words lingered...it would be different between the two of them. For a split second, Laney thought she heard those words out loud. But, no, they had only been spoken by an insistent voice in the back of her head. A strong voice. A voice that thought it knew better than she did. She and Coby would be a disaster on a date. What would they talk about? His dad's case? That would be off limits.

All she did was work, especially for the past few months. Trying to prove herself as sheriff was hard earned. The mess and distrust Skinner left for the office was taking time to clean up. Plus, her job was such a huge part of who she was and she took pride in caring for and protecting those in her county, much like the McGannon men did. When she really thought about it, they weren't so different after all. Both had enormous pride in their work. Both shared a passion for their jobs like no other. And both put their own needs on the backburner when duty called.

The world quieted in the next few seconds and all Laney could think or see was the brown of Coby's eyes. She got lost in that soft brown color, thinking how it was like looking into honey mixed with cinnamon. Clear white surrounded the soft brown hue of his irises. Thick black lashes hooded eyes she could look into all day.

In that moment, she was lost—lost in the abyss that was Coby. Lost in his strong presence. Lost in his warm spicy scent.

And for a second, all she could think about was closing the distance between them and capturing that droplet of water in the corner of his mouth.

Shaking off the fog, Laney forced her gaze onto the laptop. Coby refilled his water glass, but not until the quirk on his lips faded.

They'd been headed into a forest fire without so much as a water hose.

On the screen, she got a hit on social media for Sarah Houser. "I have something if you want to come take a look." Her voice was low, gravelly. It gave away her attraction but she couldn't be bothered with trying to cover it up now. It wasn't as if he hadn't already figured it out based on the small smirk on his lips—lips that looked even better up close.

Heat crawled up her neck and she could feel her face flush. She'd never been good at hiding an attraction, but it had never been a problem or interfered with her work before. She was pro-level at compartmentalizing, except with Coby.

He took a seat next to her and she could feel frissons of heat firing between them to the point she almost scooted her chair over to get more breathing room. But that would be silly. She was a grown woman, capable of handling a little out of control frisson of attraction.

This seemed like a good time to remind herself once this case was over, Coby would go back to his all-consuming work on the ranch and she would do the same for her job. From sun up until long past sundown, she would continue to prove herself worthy of the job she'd been elected to do. By all accounts, she was making progress on all fronts. She was winning over naysayers and converting folks who'd lost faith in the sheriff and everything the office stood for.

Acting on her attraction to Coby was out of the question. It would put her professionalism under question, especially as she was still investigating his father, and she couldn't have that. Not after all her hard work. So, when she turned toward him to speak and her throat dried up, she knew she was in trouble if she didn't stand up right away.

Like now.

No more waiting for inspiration. She needed to get to her feet and open a window maybe. Anything that would get his unique scent out of her senses.

He leaned in like he was going to whisper a secret in her ear. His lips brushed past her neck, sending sensual shivers skittering across the sensitive skin. Her breath caught. Her pulse raced. Her fingers itched to reach out to him and get lost in that thick dark mane of his.

Controlling impulses wasn't something Laney normally struggled with. And yet, here she was. Doing just that, battling for control.

And she was tired. Tired of fighting the attraction she felt toward Coby. Tired of holding back in her romantic life when she wanted to charge forward. Tired of controlling her feelings instead of letting them gallop away, free.

She sucked in a burst of air as temptation overtook logic and she closed a little more of the space in between them. Waiting for him to act because there was no way she was going to.

Or was she?

8

Coby leaned in a little closer. He took in a breath, ushering in Laney's spring flower scent. It had been a long time since he'd been this close to anyone, longer still since he'd been this near someone he could see himself really caring about. He already knew she was smart. He'd seen her compassion.

It was probably a mistake to let his lips graze her neck when he leaned in to tell her how much he appreciated her help. But he did it anyway.

Mistake be damned, he'd needed to be close to her, to feel the heat ricocheting between them. To remind himself he was still a human being who had needs—a need for connection, a need for companionship, a need to be close to another human being.

All he wanted to do was lean into the feeling.

A voice in the back of his mind reminded him that he needed to pull back. This was the sheriff, a person who was investigating his father for attempted murder. It wouldn't be her fault if she had to arrest him again. And yet, would he blame her in some way for it? Would he be able to look at her the same if she was the one who built a case against his father and then locked him behind bars?

Those thoughts were the equivalent of a bucket of ice water being tossed over his head; a cold, harsh reminder to get his act together. There were so many fish in the sea. Why was the one that was off limits the most tempting? This was a temptation he didn't need to act on, no matter how great she smelled or how much he wanted to claim those cherry lips of hers.

He needed to pull up anchor and find a new fishing spot. Period.

With some effort, he forced himself to pull back and refocus on the laptop screen. "What did you find on social media?" He could hear the gruffness in his own voice. It didn't help matters that Laney didn't immediately pull back.

After a deep breath, she turned and ran her finger over the trackpad. The screen came to life. She entered a password into the screensaver and a social media account popped onto the screen. Sarah Houser had exactly one hundred and thirty-seven friends. Who knew if those people were real friends or people she'd met online. He had no problems with either, but some might know her secrets, whereas others would only know what she chose to show them. That was the funny thing about social media, and part of the reason he didn't own an account; a person could present themselves in any way they wanted. Pictures with friends who were actually co-workers in a rare moment of togetherness. People posted those. Pictures of travel or exotic foods someone had eaten. People posted those too. Heck, people posted what they ate for breakfast, lunch, and dinner. He didn't need to know people's eating habits.

What they rarely ever posted was a picture of them

sitting alone in front of the TV on a Friday night, wishing they were somewhere else. Anywhere else.

Friends could be found on social media. He'd heard of people meeting there, getting married, and being happy. But people could present any image of themselves they wanted, and most often posted about the life they wished they had.

After work, he was too tired to sit in front of a screen all night, TV or otherwise. Yeah, he put the occasional game on, but it was more as background noise than anything else. He preferred sitting outside, looking up at the stars. Or listening to music in front of a roaring fireplace when it got cold outside.

And since he was coming clean about what he liked, he wouldn't mind taking Laney to see his home at the ranch. They could go for a walk on the property and breathe in fresh air. He'd take her back to his place and...

There his imagination went again. He lassoed his thoughts, wrangling them to the case again. The momentary distraction of Laney Justice was just that, a temporary disruption.

Laney cleared her throat. "I thought we could look at her friends and see if you recognize Jackie's picture. It might help us figure out her last name."

"Okay." He seemed to be suffering from the same dry throat she was. He got up and fixed them two glasses of water, figuring it would do them both some good to ease the dryness in their throats.

"I have coffee if you want a cup before we hit the road," she offered.

"Sounds like a winner to me." He started to get up but she stopped him with a hand on his forearm, and didn't that sent a jolt rocketing up his arm and through his body.

"You stay here. I'll make the coffee. Look at the pictures."

The words were suggestions and her voice was soft, like she'd been just as affected by contact as he was and was trying to recover.

Coby turned his attention to the laptop. He ran his finger along the trackpad to keep the system from going to sleep. First, he scrolled down Sarah's page. Recognition dawned as the impact of him recognizing her slammed into him like hitting a wall at a hundred miles an hour.

One by one, he looked through her friends' list, searching for a link.

"Does it strike you as odd that a mother and baby have gone missing, and yet no one has reported it?" he asked Laney.

"Not really. This all seems to be happening in real time. If mother and child were taken today, enough time might not have passed for someone to notice," she explained as she made coffee.

She brought a cup over and set it down next to his hand.

"I took a look at her page," he started. "She's definitely the one I saw at the party."

"Did you speak to her at all?" she asked.

"Only to ask if she needed anything," he admitted. "She said she was okay but that I was about the nicest person she'd ever met. She got emotional and I thought maybe she'd been drinking too much. Most people don't just randomly vomit and cry at a party."

"Not usually."

"It struck me as odd because her voice was fine. There was no slur in her words. Her eyes were red," he said. "She seemed more upset than sick."

"I'm wondering if maybe she'd been in a fight with the child's father. It's possible she only just found out she was pregnant."

He continued scrolling down the page, looking at entries. There weren't many. Most of them were cat memes. A post from around two months ago caught his eye. Newborn feet with what looked like ink on the bottoms. These were the tiniest feet and toes he'd ever seen in his life. He didn't understand how any parent could look at a vulnerable infant, something truly so helpless, and then just walk away to let the kid fend for itself. As if to say, *Good luck, kiddo, figure it out yourself.*

Donny wouldn't win any awards for parenting, but at least he'd cared enough to leave his kids with someone who would take care of them. As he was being reminded, not every kid got that much. Shame.

"This must be from right after the birth. Within a few hours, the hospital usually inks the feet and them stamps them on a commemorative shirt. I've seen it when I've been in the ER waiting with a dad for his kid to be born," Laney said. "Sometimes I get invited to stay and celebrate and this is one of the things the hospital does for families."

"What about you? Ever think about having one of those of your own?" he asked Laney. There was a wistful quality to her voice when she spoke about being with a newly minted family that made him wonder.

"I did at one time," she said and then the subject seemed closed when she took a sip of coffee. There was a story behind those words. Pain? She pointed to the screen in a literal redirection. "Is this your Jackie?"

He wouldn't exactly call her *his.* But, looking at the picture, he concluded this to be the woman he dated a couple of times. She was in the background of another party. The picture taken at the same lake house on Lake Travis. "That's Jackie."

"Let's see if we can identify anyone else in the picture," she said.

"Based on the date stamp, this was taken after I visited the lake house."

"Who owns the property?"

"Your guess is as good as mine. They were friends of Jackie's," he admitted.

"If we can't find her, maybe we can figure out this address."

"You don't have to do that. It should be in the memory of my GPS." He'd programmed it in when Jackie asked him to pick her up there. They were supposed to go out to a restaurant but he figured she was trying to impress him with her friends when she redirected. He squinted at the picture that filled the screen. "Any chance you can blow that up any bigger without making it so blurry I won't be able to recognize a face?"

She clicked on the picture and it filled the screen. It was pixilated and it was impossible to make out faces.

"There." He pointed at the screen. "I wish he was facing the other way. This guy seems familiar, but then again, I used to go to Austin more to listen to live music. It's likely that I've seen him around the bar circuit."

There was something strangely familiar with the dark-haired guy. From where he stood, back to the camera, it was impossible to get a good look at his face. Plus, there were others standing around, blocking a full body view even from the back.

The feeling he knew this guy niggled at the back of his mind.

～

"I'm CHECKING to see if there's any mention of a father on her page." Laney studied the pictures. She examined each face on Sarah's friend list.

"Are you getting anything to work with?" he asked.

"Nothing. We do have family names now," she said. That was something. There was no way they could call family members during this process and alert them their sister or daughter was in trouble. Laney had no idea what the perp would do if he found out contact had been made with his victim's family. Plus, they might go to the media or hire a civilian who claimed to have experience in cases like these. Those people usually claimed to be ex-military. Some actually were. Others, not so much.

"What about male friends?" he asked.

Laney opened up the friends' list and studied the faces. Out of one hundred and thirty-seven friends, only a handful were men.

"Do you get the impression this page is relatively new?" he asked.

"As a matter of fact, I do." She kept scrolling until she found the 'joined on' date. And, yes, it turned out Sarah Houser's page was new. In fact, she had only joined a year ago. "Strange that she shows up on social media around the time she got pregnant."

"Which could mean that she had a page before and deactivated it once she got pregnant," he surmised.

"Now, we just have to figure out why she would cancel her page and start a new one," she said.

"A fresh start. It's like when Miss Penny goes through her closets at the end of every year and has us do the same. She gathers up all the clothes we don't need for donation, and does the old out with the old and in with the new before New Year's."

"People also change out their page when they're trying to hide something," she added.

"Like who the baby's father is."

"My thoughts exactly," she agreed.

"Is there any way to find out what was on her old page?" he asked.

Laney chuckled. "Yes. But that would take a judge's order and you warned me not to go down that path. It would also take a while to pull it off and could run past the timeline. We're moving in that direction now, in fact."

"So, she basically put up a new page to scrub her old one." He tapped his fingers on the table. "What if Sarah Houser is a made-up name? The perp said earlier she had a different birth name," he pointed out.

"Well, that's exactly right. The perp could have been trying to throw us off the trail with the whole birth name comment early on," she said. "But if this is a fake account, Sarah Houser might be a scout. You saw a person with her likeness throwing up but you never saw a positive pregnancy test or a baby bump. Although those can be faked too."

He scrolled down the page to a post from roughly nine months ago, and, yep, there it was. A positive stick test. The post netted six likes.

"Might be time to investigate whether or not these are real friends or bots," Laney said.

"What about the picture with Jackie?"

"A crime ring would make this just believable enough for it not to be questioned," she said.

"And the baby from the text that was sent?" he asked.

"She might not exist at all. Well, that's not entirely accurate. The picture was someone's baby but that doesn't mean she was kidnapped. It could have been taken from the internet or off someone's phone."

"They provided proof of life. Are you saying that's bogus?" he asked.

"It's possible. It's so easy to manipulate pictures nowadays. Plus, we might be dealing with a criminal organization who would have resources, like graphics people. This could be an operation, which is why I need to bring in the feds. Or at least open up the investigation officially. Use all the resources I can to shut this down. This one might be bigger than the two of us can handle," she admitted. She wasn't doubting her ability as sheriff or his as a tracker. The two of them together made for one heckuva team, but she wouldn't walk into any unknown and dangerous situation without backup. Protocol was there to keep officers alive and safe.

"There's one problem," he said and she could tell by his tone of voice she wasn't going to win the battle of bringing in more resources. "What if it isn't a crime ring? What if a child's life really is in danger? What if I make the wrong move and because of that, a little girl dies?" He shook his head and fisted his right hand. "I can't live with those *what ifs*."

9

No matter how much time Coby spent staring at the screen, the flow of information had stopped with the new account. There was no doubt in his mind he was making the right choice by following the perp's instructions. All he had to do was look at the face of that little angel to know if there was a chance—no matter how slight—that she was real, his next few actions could mean the difference between life and death for her.

That was all Coby needed to know. He didn't doubt his own abilities either. He was one of the best trackers in the state, as were his brothers and cousins. He could investigate the site and change course if he got the first whiff this was an operation and not an individual.

Then there was Laney to consider. She'd done a bang up job on all the cases that she'd worked on with his family so far. She was thorough and well-respected. He respected her.

"I have to go through with this until I know otherwise." He picked up the throwaway cell and pulled up the picture of the little girl. When the angel's face filled the screen, he set the phone in front of Laney.

She seemed to realize there wasn't anything she could do to change his mind. "I'll just get dressed for the trip."

As she pushed up to standing, he put his hand up to stop her.

"I think we can sell you as my current girlfriend, especially in that outfit." His remark caused the sexiest red blush to flush the creamy skin of her cheeks. He hadn't meant to embarrass her. "I meant that as a compliment. You're beautiful."

She tilted her head to one side. "And you're just noticing that now?"

He chuckled. "No offense but I barely saw your face before. You did a good job at keeping it hidden." He paused, wondering if he should come clean or not. What the heck? They were about to get to know each other even more than before since they'd be spending the next twenty-four or so hours together. "For the record, I always thought you were pretty but it's your sharp mind that I noticed first. That, and your compassion."

"I'll take that as the compliment you intend it to be." More of that crimson color flamed her cheeks. Much more of that and he'd reach out to bring those lips closer to his and show her just how beautiful he thought she was.

Again, he had to laugh at himself. Laney Justice probably didn't need to be 'shown' anything. And she'd probably throw a punch if he acted without express permission. The irony there was that Coby hadn't wanted to act on instinct so strongly since he was a kid and had no idea what to do with all those raging hormones.

He was a grown man now and didn't give into childish actions. Real men made absolutely certain any advances were welcomed and wanted. Hell, desired was a stronger and more appropriate word choice. It was also the best word to describe his feelings toward Laney.

Again, a relationship would fizzle out pretty darn fast when he had to refer to his girlfriend as the arresting officer for his father's case. Plus, there would be even more conflicts of interests on her side. Her job was a political one and she took it seriously. Neither of them would even consider risking her livelihood for a fling, no matter how incredible the sex would be. And he was certain it would be right up there with the best sex he'd ever had. Given his past, that would take some doing.

"Do you mind going undercover for this unofficial case?" he asked, thinking he would have liked to have met her under different circumstances. There was so much possibility when he looked into those light green eyes, eyes that were glittery when they stood too close. He was certain she felt an attraction brewing between them too. As certain as the fact that stars were incredible against a velvety night sky.

"I'm classifying this as an official investigation because I can't be involved otherwise. But, no, I don't mind going undercover. And I don't mind slacking a day or two on filing the report. But, Coby, I can't continue in an unofficial capacity. I hope you understand."

Stuck between a rock and a hard place sounded about right.

If Coby didn't accept her help, the risks shot up. If he accepted her help moving forward, he was going to have to accept all that came with it. And that meant filing a report. He wasn't against the idea in total. And she had offered to delay filing a report, which was an absolute necessity. His mind was still spinning over whether or not this was an individual or a ring. An individual would be easier to overcome. A ring? A group who did nothing but target individuals like him—folks with money? There was no telling how many resources a ring would have at their disposal. More than he wanted to risk. Money was one thing. He'd hand it over in a heartbeat if it meant saving a child.

Being played for a fool? He didn't take that lightly one bit.

Reluctantly, he nodded his agreement. There wasn't really a choice to make. He needed her help, and she had a job to do. Her dilemma was valid and just as important as his predicament.

"Ready to go?" He'd taken care of Diesel's food, water, and outdoor needs.

"Are we round tripping?" she asked before saying, "never mind."

"We'll know after we get there." He was still bothered by the fact Jackie hadn't called him back or even sent a text with a middle finger sticking up at him. Either way, he'd know she was safe and hadn't been somehow sucked into this nightmare. If she was okay, he wanted answers. She might not be able to provide them, but he wanted them all the same.

A thought struck. His leverage with the perp was money. As long as he didn't have the money on him, the perp had a vested interest in him staying alive so he could make the drop tomorrow. Kill him, and any chances of reaping a reward died with him.

The thought gave him a little more comfort in dragging Laney to Austin with him. He didn't want to put her in the line of fire. And, yes, he realized how that sounded. She worked in law enforcement and was more qualified than him to deal with perps like this. But Coby was used to tracking poachers and their mindset was easier to read. He had an idea of what he was up against and had dealt with folks like them his entire life.

Laney reappeared in the hallways with an overnight bag. "I don't normally keep an emergency bag with me. This is just in case we sleep over while we're there."

He also noticed she'd slipped her shoulder holster on underneath her jacket. The more firepower the better. And even better yet that she was trained to use hers. "Let's do this."

The drive to Austin went by fast. Diesel slept in the backseat, snug as a bug in a rug. His snoring in rhythm with the sound of tires on the highway. Laney was quiet on the ride down and she seemed to be working a few things out in her mind.

Coby didn't mind the silence. He was the same way. He needed a few minutes every day to sit down away from others and process his day. It was the part about living alone that he liked best. Well, technically, he was never alone. Diesel was there. His quiet companionship was a constant for Coby. They were a pair, all right. Neither seemed to prefer the company of too many others or for too long. Laney was different. She seemed to fit right in.

Being with her didn't feel like work, as it did with so many others. He loved his brothers and cousins, he loved Miss Penny and Hawk, he loved his uncle and part of him even wanted to love Donny. But spend a day with any one of them and he was ready for solitude. Spend a week with anyone else and he was ready to go camping for a few days to recharge his battery. That's how it had always worked for him before today with the woman seated in his passenger seat. She was interesting. Spending time with her, getting to see how her mind worked, wasn't helping him dim the attraction.

Well, good. It was probably for the best someone had awakened the beating organ inside his ribcage. Jesus, he couldn't remember the last time a woman held this much appeal. Did it have something to do with the fact she was forbidden fruit?

Coby doubted it. He'd never really been the kind of person who wanted what he couldn't have. What he did have was always enough for him. He'd never been the guy who thought the grass was greener on the other side of the fence. He preferred his side of the fence just fine.

Laney had been tapping her finger on the armrest and he noticed she did that a lot when she was really concentrating. He probably shouldn't take note of her little quirks and things that made her unique. He probably shouldn't want to kiss her either, but that ship had sailed off into the distance a couple of hours ago.

"THIS IS JACKIE'S HOUSE."

Laney squinted to see the small bungalow in the darkness. They were southwest of the city, on the outskirts, and there wasn't much in terms of streetlights. The sun was almost hiding, allowing for a peek of light to filter through the trees lining the small street. Cars were parked on both sides and she held her breath half expecting Coby's Jeep to take out a rearview mirror or two as he navigated the small street.

Call him adept because he managed to skillfully slip through unscathed. She was used to driving an SUV, but she wasn't so confident she could have pulled off the maneuver. She added excellent driver to the growing list of his positive attributes.

"Someone could be keeping an eye on the place," she warned.

"Yep." He found a spot and parked. Again, she was impressed with his driving abilities. "Stay right there and I'll come get you."

He was out of the driver's side before she could question him. She quickly realized he was planning to sell this as a date when he came around to her side and opened the door for her. She was an independent woman who made her own living, depending on no one but herself, but it was nice to have the door opened for her once in a while.

Diesel loped out of the Jeep and she followed, grabbing onto Coby's extended arm and playing the game that he was her date. She ignored the electricity that caused her arm to vibrate from the point of contact. She ignored how right it felt to let someone else take the lead for once.

Coby immediately looped his arm around her shoulders after closing the door. The move was purely for display purposes, but her brain clearly didn't get the memo because it told her this was an incredibly romantic moment. Lot of help it was being. In all seriousness, Coby was exactly the kind of person she could see herself with beyond a couple of dates. She could envision snuggling up on a Friday night to watch a crackling fire outdoors and under the canopy of a night sky. She could see herself waking up with him next to her and then staying in bed on a Saturday morning long past what would be considered a reasonable time to crawl out of bed. Coffee. Breakfast. Sex. Not necessarily in that order. Preferably not in that order.

He'd gone to her left side and she quickly realized he was doing what he could to shield the fact she was carrying. Smart guy, not that she'd underestimated him. All she could think right then was that he would make one helluva deputy.

Okay, that wasn't all she could think, but it was the safest place to let her mind go to. She leaned in as close as she could to his strong frame, careful to cover her gun with her arm.

The lights were out as they approached the small chain-link fence surrounding the front yard. There was no activity on this street but there were walkers on the bigger road five houses down near where they'd parked.

At least the darkness would make it next to impossible for anyone to get a good description of either one of them. The lack of activity on the street played into their hands as well. If anything moved, it was obvious.

The U-shaped latch on the gate was easy to slide up. Coby held it open for Laney. She went in first, followed by Diesel this time. Leaving the gate open was a good tactic. It would ensure an easy exit should anything go down while they were on the cement porch.

Laney hopped up the two-stairs leading to a porch barely big enough for all three of them. She stopped long enough to take in a deep breath. It was a good sign she couldn't smell anything pungent coming from the home. But it didn't mean that they could assume that Jackie was safe either.

The lack of a response to Coby's call was troublesome. If Jackie was the clingy type—the type who would misread signals her date was losing interest—she would have responded by now. The words, *if she was able,* were true but not exactly reassuring.

Coby glanced at her. It was too dark outside to see his eyes clearly and hers hadn't adjusted to the lack of light.

He opened the metal screen door and knocked. Three

solid raps. Nothing but quiet. He repeated the action. More quiet. The only noise was the sound of him knocking for a third time. He knocked hard, like police raid hard.

"I'll see if I can get a look through a window," he said and she said put her arm up to stop him.

"I can't go with you," she warned. "I still have to follow protocol."

Laney stayed on the front porch, arms crossed over her chest. The move was made to look like she was cold, but in reality she was keeping her hand closer to her gun. Every second counted in a situation that went south fast. This, like many other cases, had the potential.

Diesel stood at her side, providing a strange amount of comfort as she shivered against the chilly air. Her jacket was too thin despite the temperatures in Austin always seeming to be a few degrees warmer than Cattle Cove. She'd dressed for the weather she thought she was going to have. And, in all honesty, wouldn't be wearing a minidress in this weather if not for the date rouse.

It was a good reminder of how quickly Texas weather could change and how chilly it could get. His idea about leaving a backpack or duffel bag in his Jeep at all times to be ready for when 'whatever' happened—which was more common than it should be—was seeming smarter and smarter with every whip of wind.

She slowly surveyed the area, playing the date role as best as she could. She could barely recall the last date she'd been on, let alone the last really good date she'd had. Since forcing that memory would just be depressing, she vowed to rethink her long hours at work and carve out some time for a social life.

Funny that it had taken meeting Coby and getting to know him, that had her examining her lack of a social life.

She was dedicated to her job, but that was only part of the reason. It had been easy to dive into work after finding out she would never bear children of her own. Wasn't that what people considered the point of marriage? To start a family?

Apparently, she had an abnormality called polycystic ovary syndrome or PCOS. Basically, it amounted to a lack of ability for her body to ovulate. She had a hormonal imbalance that resulted in a whole lot of small cysts on her ovaries. Her irregular cycles and inconvenient acne weren't things she even knew she should have checked out. No one talked about those things in her house. What she knew about starting her period for the first time was information passed along by well-meaning friends. She'd picked up bits and pieces of information here and there. Her mother was from a generation of women who just didn't discuss anything 'female' related.

Laney didn't blame her mother for the condition getting out of control. Her mother couldn't have known this would happen. But since starting a family normally followed marriage for most couples, and she knew straight out of the gate that wasn't going to be an option for her, she'd shelved the whole marriage idea in favor of a career.

And, yes, she could be a little bit extreme when she really dug into an idea. She'd gone all-in with her career and was one of the youngest sheriffs in the state.

Avoiding the thought of marriage and family altogether had made it real easy to find fault with everyone she dated. There was no doubt in her mind that Coby was special. A relationship with him would be special. She was also becoming aware that maybe she'd done so to avoid the whole *I can't have kids* conversation if the relationship started looking like something that could last. Because that conversation was a devastating one to have, especially when she didn't know whether it would be a deal breaker for the other person.

Wow. Standing on a cold porch at night in Austin was suddenly therapeutic. Her mind also had a tendency to wander when she was on stakeouts. The eyes stayed sharp and on target while the mind went into territory she normally avoided. There was something about being in absolute quiet, absolute stillness, that made her mind become reflective. Maybe that was the reason so many people stuck to crowded places, avoiding being alone at all costs.

She didn't mind alone. But, now, she was beginning to see just how alone she'd become. Could she open up her life and her heart a little bit to someone?

Her mind wanted to make a case for that 'someone' to be Coby, but he was absolutely off limits.

10

"No one is home." Coby returned to the front of the house. Relief washed over him at the sight of Laney. Being away from her, not knowing if anything had happened to her was a gut punch. In fact, he worried.

More than a few times in the past several minutes he'd had to remind himself that she worked in law enforcement and was probably more, if not equally, as competent with a gun as he was. His pride didn't want to admit he could be outshot by anyone, no matter how skilled a marksman he was up against. So, he would leave that thought alone and not tempt fate by asking outright.

"It's possible she's at the lake house," she offered, standing on the porch, rubbing her hands up and down her arms to stave off the cold.

"My thoughts exactly," he said as he approached. "May I put my arm around you?"

She looked a little bit surprised at the question and he immediately knew the reason. He hadn't asked permission when he'd done it before. This time meant a little more than show to him, despite trying to deny it.

"Yes." The small smile that tugged at the corners of her lips caused his chest to squeeze. It was probably a good thing dating her was out of the question on so many levels. Probably.

Back in the Jeep, they each settled into their seats as Diesel made himself comfortable in the back. Coby pulled up the address to the lake house on his GPS system. The house wasn't too far from Jackie's place. His sense of unease increased two-fold with every mile they got closer to the party house. And the party was still going. Cars lined the street and music thumped as he rolled down the windows to listen.

Voices carried, as did laughter. The place was definitely hopping. He wondered how many people in a situation like this just paid the ransom. Would it end there? Had he been tagged as some kind of millionaire playboy? Because reality was the opposite. He dated around and spent time with plenty of women but he'd never consider himself a womanizer. He would never lower himself or have that little respect for women. It just wasn't part of his character. And even if it had been, Miss Penny would have seen to it the trait was gone before she let him walk out of the house.

Paying a ransom for a child who couldn't possibly belong to him ranked right up there with burning money on trash day. Paying a ransom to save a life was another issue altogether.

"What are you thinking about?" Laney asked and he suddenly realized she'd been studying him.

"I'm just wondering what kind of person I've been pegged as," he said.

"How so?"

"It seems like I've been lumped into a category of people who wouldn't know if he'd fathered a child or not," he said.

"Mistakes happen, Coby."

"Do you know that from personal experience?" he asked a little too quickly. The minute those words left his mouth, he wished he could reel them back in. "Don't answer that. Your personal life isn't any of my business."

"It could be," she said. There was no hint of judgment in her tone, making him feel like a real jerk.

"This situation is stressful and I said those words without thinking. You should know something about me. I'm not perfect," he started, by way of a better apology. "But I admit when I'm in the wrong. And that was a jerk move."

"Yes," she said calmly. "It was."

"Will you accept my apology?" His heart hammered inside his chest. Her answer meant more to him than he wanted to let on.

"Yes. But, Coby, that doesn't mean I'll put up with it again."

"You shouldn't have to," he said with the conviction he felt. "And, for the record, I would very much like to know more about you."

"Well, then, I'll start with telling you there hasn't been a pregnancy scare in my life, ever, because I can't have children." With that, she opened the Jeep door and got out.

This was one of those situations where he wasn't sure if he should stay in the vehicle or follow. But she'd just bared a piece of her soul and he couldn't let her get away without knowing how much he appreciated her trust.

So, he hopped out and told Diesel to stay put. The windows were open and the air was cool, so he would be comfortable. Besides, he was on his favorite blanket looking like he'd rather be asleep, and he thought that Laney would appreciate not having a dog distracting him whilst he talked to her. She'd shown him her vulnerabilities, the least he could do was be there for her.

"Good boy," he reassured before joining Laney at the front of his Jeep.

She stood there, arms crossed over her chest, legs crossed at the ankles, looking up at the stars. It was an especially beautiful night even by the strictest standards. He walked over to her, side-by-side, and stared up.

"It took a lot of courage for you to tell me something that personal, Laney." Seeing her as a real person and not just a uniform made him wish he knew more about her. "Thank you for trusting me."

She leaned into his arm with her shoulder. "I figure we've learned more about each other in the past few hours than most people know after months of dating. So, you're welcome. Besides, I know more about you than you know about me. That seemed lopsided."

She turned to face him, and her smile caused his gut to clench. Yeah, he was in trouble. Not so much that he couldn't dig his way out. At least, he hoped.

He brought his hand up to her face, lazily running his finger along her jawline. He clenched his back teeth and smiled at the pain being this close to her without being able to really touch her was causing him.

"What's our next move?" she asked with glittery eyes.

He didn't immediately have an answer. At least, not one he could share with her.

Voices interrupted the moment. He glanced over her shoulder and saw a small pack of ladies walking in their direction.

"May I kiss you?" His gaze bounced from the ladies to Laney and back, privately grateful for the excuse to ask.

She followed his eyes.

"Permission granted." Before he could make a move, she'd grabbed a fistful of his shirt and was tugging him toward her. Her back was to the ladies, so he repositioned so she could keep an eye on them. But make no mistake about it when his lips found hers, all rational thought escaped him. All he could think about was how soft her full cherry lips were when they moved against his. How good she smelled with her flowers in spring scent as it filled his senses. And how much he felt like he was exactly where he belonged for the first time in his life.

Getting lost in the feeling was hazardous, so he forced himself to listen to see if he could pick up anything in the ladies' conversation as they passed by.

Their words became whispers and he opened his eyes long enough to see them stagger away from him and Laney, like they were giving them privacy. This was the reaction he'd been hoping for from them when he'd initiated the kiss, but he no longer wanted to focus on anything but Laney. He brought his right hand up, tunneling his fingers in her hair to better position her mouth as he claimed it with more force this time.

She reacted by bringing her hands up to his shoulders, where her fingernails dug into him. Her actions did little more than egg him on. All he could think was that he wanted more. More of the kiss. More of her skin against his. More of her...period.

~

LANEY HAD to dig deep to find the strength to pull back. She had never been so thoroughly kissed in her entire life. She finally understood the reference to weak knees and curled toes.

Risking a glance at Coby, she had a small sense of satisfaction the kiss seemed to have the same effect on him. Looking into those gorgeous brown eyes, she saw a storm brewing like none she'd ever experienced.

It took her a few seconds to break through the fog and think clearly again.

At least now, she knew what to look for in her next kiss. The bar by which all others would be measure had been raised to new heights. And that was a good thing...right?

"What's our next move?" Coby asked, his deep timbre gravelly. Sexy.

She turned toward the house and took in the scene. People were coming and going freely, and yet Coby showing up could raise a red flag. "No one knows me, so I might want to take a lap around to see what I can pick up. What was your impression the last time you were here? Is this a close-knit circle or random people and hookups?"

"I got the impression there were both. A few mainstays and then a whole lot of people bringing dates, like in the case of myself and Jackie," he admitted.

His gaze fixed on something or someone off her left shoulder.

"Should I turn around or stay put?" she asked.

"Jackie."

"Excuse me," she said, wondering why he'd repeated the name. And then it dawned on her. "She's who you're staring at, isn't she?"

"Yes." His lips thinned and his gaze narrowed.

"Confronting her while we're here will alert everyone to our presence," she felt the need to point out.

"We don't want that," he said. "I'm just more concerned with checking that she's all right."

"So, I have a question that might seem a little out there. Bear with me."

He nodded.

"Did you actually *watch* her polish off a bottle of wine? Or did you assume she was the one who finished it?" There was a difference. Subtle but important. It was a lot like when someone ordered a 'Gibson in disguise.' Basically a non-alcoholic drink masking as a real bar drink. Clearly, he'd ordered the wine but that didn't mean she drank it all. Laney had friends in college who routinely tossed a shot on the floor or over their shoulder when their bar mates weren't looking because they wanted to seem part of the fun but had hit their alcohol limit.

His gaze unfocused like he was looking inside himself for the answer.

"As a matter of fact, I always saw a glass in her hand and I can attest to the occasional sip, but my opinion is based on the empty bottle and her behavior as the night went on. Her behavior changed in proportion to how much wine was left. So, no, I didn't actually see her take the entire bottle down now that you mention it."

"It's possible, then, that she was acting the whole time," she said.

The storm changed course in his eyes and intensified. "That, it is."

His nostrils flared and he flexed and released his fingers a couple of times like he was trying to keep them from fisting. Betrayal was a bitter pill. She'd come across it in her job more times than she could count. She'd felt it in her personal life too. Her body refusing to perform the most basic of human functions, reproduction, felt like the worst betrayal.

So, yeah, she recognized the look. She'd seen it staring back at her in the mirror.

She also trusted him to lead with logic and not emotions. Too many people couldn't do that, but Coby was different, remarkable, in so many more ways than one. The more time she spent around him, the better he got. He saw the long game and wouldn't blow it.

"She just grabbed a guy's arm to steady herself," he said low and under his breath.

She closed some of the distance between them and then brought her hands up to loop around his neck, locking her fingers. The earth tilted on its axis but she forced herself to stay focused on the case.

"Now, she's smiling at him and swaying just a little. I have to say he doesn't seem as annoyed by it as I was," he admitted. "Now, they're getting into his car. Sports car. Red."

"Do you recognize him?" she asked.

"Maybe." His gaze narrowed again like he was reading the fine print on a contract. "He looks familiar."

"Rich?"

"His sports car would give that impression. But, he looks like an athlete. Showy with his money. Specialized plates."

"Pull your cell out of your pocket," she instructed, staring at those brown eyes, trying not to give into how they affected her.

He did. She grabbed it and held it up like she was taking a close-up of him. Instead, she turned the camera around and shot a pic of the red sports car.

"That way, I can run the plates when we get home." The word, *home*, rolled off her tongue so easily, and yet what she meant to say was Cattle Cove.

She handed the cell back to him but not before sending the photo to her phone first. It was more secure that way in case something happened to either one of them.

"Why don't I take a lap around, while you stay here with Diesel?" she said.

"And if something happens to you inside?" There was a protective quality to his voice that gave her stomach a free-falling sensation, like she'd just base jumped from the top of a mountain.

"I'll be okay. If I get in trouble, I'll find a safe place and text you," she said.

"Or we could go together and skip going inside. We could grab a boat off the dock and get closer via the water," he offered.

"Good idea and one we might use for surveillance after I figure out who we might want to be taking a closer look at." Looking into those tortured eyes, she felt the need to add, "Trust me. This is what I do for a living. It sometimes puts me in dangerous situations but I know how to be careful. I know when to make an exit and my badge is in my purse should the need arise."

"Which is a good point. Are you allowed to just walk onto someone's private property without permission? Would anything you learn still be admissible in court?" His questions were on target.

"Going undercover doesn't mean walking up to the door and knocking. Yes, I have to be invited, and no, I don't have to identify myself since I'm not here on official business. I'm here to use the restroom and anything I see while I'm inside might be classified as illegal. But, no, that's not why I'm going inside. I don't think I'm going to be arresting anyone in particular. This is information gathering. I'm out on a date and I need to pee. It's as simple as that."

She moved to where she could get a good look at herself in the Jeep's rearview mirror. She finger-combed her hair and checked her face. She grabbed red lipstick from her purse and touched up her mouth.

When she turned toward Coby, he captured her wrist in his hand. His touch was gentle as he brought her hand up to his lips and feathered a kiss on the tender skin of her wrist.

"Be careful." The storm raged as he made eye contact with her, locking gazes. "You've become important to me."

11

The eleven minutes Laney was out of sight were the longest of Coby's life. He'd hopped inside his Jeep and waited. Each minute was excruciating. The only comfort he had was in the knowledge she knew what she was doing and was damn good at her job.

Laney had proven time and time again that she knew how to handle herself in any situation. Logic said she'd be fine. Tell his heart that, though.

Coby didn't normally do 'emotion' when it came to others. He was more the 'live and let live' type. As long as no one was infringing on anyone else's freedoms or ability to earn a living, folks had a right to pursue whatever happiness meant to them.

So, it caught him off guard that all his protective instincts flared as he watched Laney walk toward the house. Since it was a party house, and definitely not his scene, he liked her going there even less.

But what if this place had ties to an extortion ring?

Again, he wondered what kind of person paid the

ransom to 'free' a mother and child who would then—
what?—promise to leave him alone?

It was brilliant actually, because most rich party guys
would be more than happy to write a check to make what
they would view as a 'situation' go away. When it came to
Coby, someone didn't do their homework.

Was it Jackie's job to scout potential suckers?

Coby watched the house through the rearview mirror,
thinking how satisfying it would be to go inside and bust up
the party. To unleash hell and let them know what he really
thought of their operation.

Of course, the homeowners could be none the wiser
about what was really going on. They might be innocent
people who liked to host parties and meet new people. It
wasn't unthinkable. People bought lake houses and beach
houses for just such purposes. Call him a country boy but
Austin was a little too crowded for his taste to think about
ever living there. A weekend was about all he could take of
the long lines for good food and traffic that knew no end to
rush hour.

No wonder he'd grown tired of coming here. Austin was
a great city, don't get him wrong. The live music was out of
this world. But he wasn't cut out for the lifestyle. The hordes
of students walking downtown at all hours of the day and
night didn't hold much appeal either.

His pulse was working double time with each passing
minute. His imagination was already working overtime, so
he did his level best to rein it in. Laney was a fine sheriff.
She was the highest caliber, top-shelf. He palmed his phone
and checked for a message.

His brothers and cousins were working overtime,
sending texts but there was still nothing from Laney. He told
himself that was probably a good thing. In the meantime, he

had to battle every instinct he had to stomp in the house and see what was going on for himself.

And then he caught a glimpse of her. His chest squeezed as the wind toyed with her long locks. She brought up a hand to move it away from her face when his pulse kicked up for a whole different reason. A man was jogging up behind her, his gaze laser-focused on Laney.

Coby immediately reached for the door handle. Stopped himself an inch from grasping the chrome fixture. He forced himself to wait and see.

The guy had on black slacks and a white button-down shirt. His sleeves were rolled up. He reached up and tapped Laney on the shoulder as Coby situated his camera phone to grab a picture of the guy. Taking a page out of Laney's playbook, Coby snapped the shot. If nothing else, they had an image.

Black Slacks would probably be considered good-looking by most standards. He was on the tall side with a runner's build. It was harder to get a good look at the details of his face from this distance. Laney, no doubt, would be paying attention.

Every muscle in Coby's body chorded, pulling tighter than overstrung piano keys ready to snap from too much tension. He reminded himself to slow it down. Laney didn't look like she was in trouble.

He did, however, see her shaking her head. Her back was to him but he could see by her stance that she'd folded her arms over her chest. Was she hiding her weapon? Good move. The thought occurred to him that she might also be making sure her trigger hand could be close enough to her weapon should the need arise.

Black Slacks shifted his weight from one side to the other, suddenly looking more like an awkward teenager than a confident adult. The reason slammed into Coby like a spray of bullets. Black Slacks was asking Laney out for a date.

Coby had no right to be jealous. Yet, he was.

He had no right to watch those two like his life depended on it. Yet, he did.

He had no right to care about her response. Yet, he did.

He cared more than he wanted to admit to her, and a helluva lot more than he wanted to admit to himself. Yet, he stayed glued to the rearview like he was watching the year's most intense drama unfold on the big screen.

So much for containing his emotions. Did he like Laney more than he wanted to admit? The answer was clear. Yes.

He exhaled as he watched Black Slacks' shoulders sag as Laney turned to walk away from him. She dropped her hands, casually swinging them at her sides like she had all the time in the world.

Coby had half a mind to step out of the Jeep to greet her to make sure Black Slacks saw that someone was waiting for her. But he didn't know what excuse she'd given and, based on her expression, she wasn't too concerned about the guy following her.

He stood there with a sappy, forlorn look. And then, he shrugged before giving her one last look as she neared the Jeep. Black Slacks disappeared as Laney passed the Jeep. Clearly, she didn't want him to know which vehicle she was getting into, so he didn't blow her cover.

This was probably a good sign in the grand scheme of things, meaning her voyage in the house was productive. She didn't give herself away and, maybe, she was able to pick up some information to help with the investigation.

Laney ducked in between two vehicles and stayed out of view for at least a minute. Coby couldn't be certain Black

Slacks wasn't standing off to the side, out of view, so he gripped the steering wheel until his knuckles went white and waited.

Seeing Laney come down the sidewalk on the driver's side was the first time he really exhaled. Black Slacks was nowhere to be seen, so they should be safe on that front. She rounded the back of the Jeep casually and then slipped inside the vehicle drawing the least amount of attention possible.

Her movements, a well-rehearsed dance. He was in awe of her. And he was also in trouble because of it.

"That was the worst eleven minutes of my life," he said to her. Relief that she was safe was a flood to dry soil.

This time, she didn't blush. She reached over and touched his arm.

"Jackie is probably a scout."

∽

"SHE THOUGHT I would be an easy mark?"

Laney couldn't see how anyone would peg a McGannon for a sitting duck. "It's beyond me why anyone would think that. She clearly didn't do her homework when it came to a McGannon. Especially with you."

"She wouldn't be the first person to try to snatch a piece of the McGannon fortune without working for it." He issued a sharp sigh. "The question now is what to do about it."

"My gut tells me that we're working with a small operation. There's one, maybe two scouts and a couple of people on the backend. Jackie and Sarah, if that's her real name, might not even know they're working together," she said.

"They didn't seem friendly with each other. Of course, that could have been all for show."

She nodded, thinking those two were fools for trying to play someone like Coby. "Jackie has moved on. It's most likely why she didn't call you back. Do you remember how the two of you met?"

"That's easy. We met at a bar on Sixth Street. Small place that has local talent. A fair amount of bands have gone on to make it on a national stage after playing the venue," he said.

"I know the place." She snapped her fingers. "I just can't think of the name. Shoot. It's on the tip of my tongue."

"Cedar Street Courtyard is the stage where the bands play, and there are a lot of places to sit outside, buy a drink, and listen."

"That's right."

He cocked an eyebrow. "You've been there?"

"A couple of times. Why are you so shocked?" She wasn't sure if she should be offended or not based on his reaction.

He shrugged as he started up the engine.

"Seriously. Tell me." Now, she needed to know.

"I don't know. It's hard to see someone like you sitting outside, relaxing, and enjoying live music while sipping on a beer. That's all," he said.

"And why is that? I'm a normal person." She heard the defensiveness in her own voice. She couldn't help herself.

"You're the sheriff. And a damn fine one. I just don't see you sitting around and relaxing is all," he said. Then, he quietly added, "And there's nothing *normal* about you."

"What does that even mean?" She probably wasn't supposed to hear what he said, let alone respond. But there she was hearing and responding.

He navigated out of the neighborhood and onto a main road leading back toward the highway.

"Nothing bad," he explained. "All I'm saying is that I see

you for work and don't think about how you must be on your time off."

It was like a balloon deflated in her chest as she exhaled. "Well, that's probably because I don't take much time off. Otherwise, people might actually see me as human and not some kind of machine."

"Hold on there. I didn't say you were a machine. Believe me when I say I'm not nearly as fond of those as I am of you," he admitted.

Those words definitely softened the blow of his earlier ones.

"It's my fault," she said. "I'm always working, always in uniform. It's half the reason I dressed up today. I'm so tired of wearing the color tan that I dressed up to go to the feed store."

He chuckled and then seemed to check himself so as not to offend her again. "It's okay for me to laugh at that, right?"

She laughed too.

"It would be even funnier if it wasn't so sad. I literally work all the time," she said.

"I do the same, so you won't be judged by me." There was something comforting in those words. "And for the record, there's nothing wrong with being dedicated to your job. You are the best sheriff we've had in ages. You should be proud of that."

"I am," she said, letting those words sink in. He was right. There was a time to work nonstop and a time to slow down and recharge. "Lately, crime has been keeping me hopping in Cattle Cove. But, I volunteer to work when my deputies could handle an assignment. I feel personally responsible to give honor back to the office after the former sheriff."

She didn't say Skinner but they both knew who she was talking about.

"For the record, I think you have done that in spades."

"Thank you," she said, and meant it. She brought her hands up to rub her temples as a tension headache was trying to take hold. "But, man, I do need to learn how to relax again. My shoulders are in knots half the time and I basically live my work."

"You care. That's a good thing," he said. "But so is taking time off."

"I can only imagine the pressure you guys work under. You're working on a family legacy." She'd thought about it a few times after getting to know the McGannons. There was a lot of pressure on each of them to do their part.

"It's different when you grow up with it. I wouldn't know any different. And, despite recent events, we're close to each other so I've always loved being on the ranch. Working with my family is one of the perks if you ask me. I get plenty of time on my own when I'm running fences. It's a large property, so we all tend to spread out and take care of business. Until recently, we always came back for Sunday supper. There's a good chunk of the year when we all work more closely."

"Calving season?" she asked, figuring that's what he was talking about. From everything she knew about cattle ranchers, they worked twenty-four-seven when all the baby calves were being born. This was especially true of a large ranch like McGannon Herd.

"That's right," he said.

"Can I ask a personal question?" She didn't want to overstep her bounds, but they'd been sharing a lot of personal stories and she found herself wanting to know even more about him.

"First off, where are we headed?"

"Depends. I think we're done here. What do you think?" she asked.

"I'm good. If I'm honest, part of me wants to follow Jackie and give her a piece of my mind, but that won't help the current situation," he admitted.

"That's true and no one would blame you for feeling that way."

"Then, I guess we're heading back to your place," he confirmed. He put on his blinker and then changed lanes. "What was it that you wanted to ask me?"

"What's your relationship like with your father?"

12

As far as questions went, Laney's got straight to the point. She deserved an equally honest and straight forward answer.

"I don't have one," Coby said point-blank.

"What has it been like since he came back last year?" she probed. "And, I'm not asking as an investigator in case you were wondering. I'm curious about it as your friend."

"Are we? Friends?" Better yet, why was he disappointed in the classification?

"I hope so. In Cattle Cove, I know a lot of people but I don't have many who I can call friends. I'm hoping to change that in the near future and I'd like it even better if I could start with you." There was a vulnerability to her voice that flared more of his protective instincts. Before the last twenty-four hours, he'd heard compassion in her voice but always strength. This new vulnerability was the ultimate strength, in his opinion. It took a helluva lot of guts to open up to others.

"Well that makes two of us," he said. "Or should I say that a whole lot of people know my family and me, at least on the surface. They think they know who we are as individuals, but they don't. If anything, it makes us hold onto what makes us unique even more. Refuse to let others see it."

"I feel the same way. Like you're saying. Everyone knows me as the sheriff. I think I've been building a solid reputation. At least, that's the hope," she said.

"You are," he reassured. He wanted her to know her efforts weren't in vain. Folks in town didn't have a bad word to say about her, despite their reservations they had about the office she held, especially after the revelations about Skinner had come to light.

"I realize your dad walked out on your family and that had to be incredibly hard for a kid to understand," she began, pensive, like there was a lot more to the story.

Did he want to know? The town must have really had a field day after Donny McGannon, the screw up between two brothers, ditched his kids.

He didn't say much of anything and she must've taken that as a sign to continue.

"My dad used to know yours."

"I didn't realize that." There was probably a whole lot he didn't know about his father's life, considering he'd never been inclined to ask.

"He said your dad didn't do so well after your mother died. It shredded him into pieces." She glanced over at him as he tightened his grip on the steering wheel.

"Go on," he urged. Her story was a like a train wreck. He couldn't bring himself to look away.

"I'm not defending him in any way, so..." She paused for a few seconds. "...don't take this the wrong way."

He nodded, reserving judgment until he heard what she had to say.

"It's just he didn't think he could bring up you boys

without her. She was basically the center of his world and the family," she said.

"So, what? He just gave up after she died. Didn't he think we needed him even more? We were kids for Chrissake."

"I'm not defending his actions," she said quickly.

He issued a sharp sigh.

"I just know that my dad believed he loved you guys enough to walk away. Said he didn't want to screw you guys up because your mother wouldn't like it. He told my father the best bet for all of you guys was not to have him in your lives. So, he took off. He called my dad a couple of times after that to check on you guys. My dad always seemed down after the calls. I heard him trying to convince your dad to come back. For what it's worth, he just didn't think he could do right by you."

"So, he hid out in a casino?" It was more statement than question.

"I think he tried to run from his emotions and distract himself," she said. "The man who came home isn't anything like the one who left all those years ago. He was heartbroken then, but still a decent person. Now, he just seems...broken."

He certainly left a path of destruction in his wake. Although, to be fair, he did leave his boys with an amazing surrogate father. Uncle Clive had stepped in and stepped up in a big way. He also never once bad-mouthed his brother. The only thing he ever said was that their father would be there with them if he could.

And now that Uncle Clive had been the one to bail his brother out of jail, Coby couldn't help but wonder if Uncle Clive knew his brother better than his sons ever would.

"Can I ask you a question?" It was his turn.

"I'll answer if I can."

"Why did you arrest my father?"

He saw her sit up a little straighter in the seat. She tested her seatbelt before taking in a slow breath. "He met with a lawyer to see if he could challenge Clive McGannon for a bigger stake in the ranch. The lawyer wasn't exactly on the up and up."

"What honest lawyer would take on a case against my uncle?" he asked.

"Exactly. What your dad didn't seem to realize was this lawyer took the meeting as a request to put a hit on your uncle. Of course, your father denied knowledge but was arrested because of it," she said. "Your uncle can't remember if anyone was in the equipment building next to him the morning of his fall. With the head injury, he seems to have lost some of his memory or blocked it all out as happens with some trauma patients."

"Basically, as soon as your father found out what he'd done, he tried to meet with the guy to straighten out the situation. At least, that's his side of the story. I'm in the process of getting a subpoena for all of the shady lawyer's records. What I'm hearing so far from a few other of this guy's 'clients' corroborates your father's story. I went to the judge with this information and he agreed to set bail pending an inquiry."

"You went to bat for my father?" He couldn't hide the shock in his voice if he'd tried.

"I went to bat for justice. I will always go to bat for justice. It's just a bonus that it might end up helping an old friend of my father's."

Coby wanted to believe there was something good left in his father.

"For what it's worth, he told my dad that leaving his boys was the worst mistake of his life."

"And your dad believes him?" They were almost to her

house by the time the conversation started winding down. Coby needed a few minutes to unplug and process everything he'd just heard. Because his mind was changing toward his father, and so was his heart.

"Yes. And so do I," she admitted.

"Thank you for telling me."

"For the record, I wanted to tell all of you at one time. With two of your brothers taking off like they did with very little warning, I had a change of plans. But I was planning to tell you guys sooner rather than later."

"Does my uncle know all this?" he asked. Now, he wondered if this was why Uncle Clive had been trying to call the family together to share a meal. He'd said he had news. Did he want to be the one to tell them?

"I'm pretty certain it's the reason he stepped up to post bail," she said. "I'm probably out of line being the one to tell you all this. Not in a professional sense, just respecting your uncle's preferences. I just think you deserve to know."

Coby nodded, relaxing his grip on the steering wheel. He took the highway exit and made the rest of the ten minute drive to her place in silence.

"I need to let the others know," he said, pulling up in front of her house. "Mind if I meet you inside in a few?"

"Not at all."

LANEY PACED inside her small kitchen. She didn't regret her decision to tell Coby. After hearing him talk about his father, he needed to know where the case stood. She still needed to get absolute proof of his innocence and would follow the evidence, wherever it led. And she would continue to be objective. She was realizing she could separate her work from her personal life, and that it was important to have one. Because, man, job burnout wouldn't make her a better investigator and she was dangerously close to walking the line.

As to the current investigation, dealing with a small operation was good. The fact the perp was targeting socially significant persons, meant he was looking for low-hanging fruit, easy pickings, the kind of person who would be willing to pay to make someone go away and keep their name out of the press.

Being in the bar scene in Austin seemed to be the connection for Coby, the reason he was targeted. That, and his family's reputation—a reputation the perp figured Coby would be willing to pay to protect.

It struck her as funny that public perception could be so off track. The McGannons were honorable men because they cared about living by a code. It didn't make them perfect or take away the mistakes they made.

It was possible the perp thought this might be a good time to strike the family considering the bad press Donny's case was getting. Maybe they thought the McGannons would be willing to do almost anything to keep their reputation from taking another hit.

A couple of quick raps at the back door was followed by Coby stepping in the kitchen. He walked inside with Diesel closely behind. Her heart squeezed. She could seriously get used to those two walking into her place like they belonged.

"How'd it go?" she asked, moving to the coffee maker to fix a couple of cups. Sleep wasn't happening tonight. They needed to come up with a strategy to catch the perp.

"They were relieved. Same as me," he admitted. "We're meeting up next weekend to have a meal together, him included. The guys are arranging it."

"That's good." It might sound corny, but the main reason she'd gone into law enforcement was to serve others. To bring justice to those who would harm another. To protect a way of life she'd grown up with and loved more than words could explain.

A little voice reminded her that she deserved to have the kind of life worth preserving too. Had she gotten a little too comfortable standing on the outskirts looking in? Had she given up hope on ever finding someone who would love her flaws and all? Who would accept the fact she could never have children?

The area where she lived was all about family, kids, and had always been that way. It had always been her plan too.

But, life didn't always cooperate. Maybe it was time to redefine her views of what made a family. She hadn't even thought about adopting until now. She didn't need a husband to have a family. A little voice in the back of her mind that was far wiser than she picked that moment to remind her the right man for her would love her no matter what.

A sense of peace settled over her at the realization.

Coby went to work refilling Diesel's water bowl.

"I have a couple of blankets in the hall closet we can set up on the floor, but he's welcome to curl up on the sofa if he'd be more comfortable there," she offered. "Whatever you let him do at home is fine with me."

"I'd hate for him to get hair all over your clean sofa," he said.

"I never wanted to live in a museum. The place is only this clean and everything is perfectly in place because, quite frankly, I'm never home. But that's about to change."

"Really? How so?"

"Work-life balance. I need to get some of that," she said with a smile.

He returned the smile and her heart melted a little bit more. Shame, she thought, to find someone who was exactly her type but would have very different life goals. Coby McGannon would want children of his own. At least now she had a blueprint of her perfect man to work from. That was more than she'd had a day ago.

"A lot of my old beliefs are changing lately," he said. "Crazy life events have a way of forcing you into a gut check. What's the cause of your change of heart?"

"You," she said under her breath. And then she said louder so he could hear, "Job burnout."

"It's been busier than usual in recent months. My family seems to have something to do with the uptick in crime," he said. "You've been amazing. We owe a huge debt of gratitude to you for everything you're doing for us. And that's especially true for me."

He walked over to her and stopped within inches. The man was temptation on a stick.

She knew one thing was absolutely certain. If she let things go any further between them, and the way he looked at her said it was possible, her heart would shatter when he walked away. And he would.

Whatever was happening between them wouldn't last no matter how much her heart wanted to argue the opposite.

13

"Is there even a baby involved at all?" Coby's plans in the next twelve hours hinged on the answer to that question.

"That much, we don't know." No matter how appreciated, Laney's honesty didn't make it any easier to move forward.

"What is the most likely scenario?" he asked.

"First things first, let's check out the photos and see if we can glean a picture from there. The more information I have to work with, the better."

He followed her to the kitchen table, where she booted up her laptop. An idea was already clicking into place in his mind. Whether there was a child involved or not, he couldn't let this jerk walk away scot-free knowing he wouldn't stop here. The perp would move onto his next victim. There was no way Coby could let that happen if he had a remote chance of stopping it.

"The picture is too blurry to get a license plate when I blow it up," Laney said.

"I figured as much."

"But this guy looks very familiar," she continued.

"Is he Bobby Barrera?" The name finally came to Coby.

"The baseball player?" She entered his name into a popular search engine.

Bingo.

"It sure is. Good catch," she said with a hint of admiration in her voice.

The irony of her comment made him smile despite the circumstances. Bobby Barrera was, in fact, a catcher.

"Well, he's next on Jackie's list. I'm guessing she scouts for or is given a mark. Then, she figures out the person's habits and shows up there a few times. Attracts the mark's attention. Once he asks her out, she finds out information to use against him," he surmised.

"My thoughts exactly," she said.

"I'm not a huge playboy. I'm wondering why they thought I'd be a good target."

"It could be as simple as all the bad press your family has been getting lately. You're single. Good looking beyond reason. You date around but you're really open about the fact you aren't getting attached to anyone. It's pretty much the playboy MO." Laney blinked up at him. "I'm not saying that's a bad thing or that it's true in your case. I can see how it would be interpreted by someone who doesn't know you like I do."

He took a minute to chew on that while she returned to the laptop. He also took note of her comment about him being good looking beyond reason, and his chest swelled more than he should allow.

"I was hoping to get a plate but we can work without it."

"What about the owner of the home? Did you speak to him?" he asked.

"He's not involved," she dismissed the idea quickly.

"How can you be so sure?"

"The guy who chased me outside...he owns the place. He was pretty clueless if you ask me." In her line of work, she would have to learn to size people up pretty quickly. Her judgment had been spot-on so far.

"What did he want from you?" There was a hint of jealousy in his voice despite his best efforts to disguise it.

"My number," she said without looking up.

"Did you give it to him?" He had no right to ask that question despite feeling the opposite.

"Why would I? I was undercover in an investigation to a crime ring happening right under the guy's nose. First of all, he might be good at making money but he wasn't sharp enough to have a real conversation with. It didn't take long to figure that out. Secondly, he's not my type. Thirdly..." She stopped right there and exhaled. "Well, that's none of your business."

He didn't like being told the last part no matter true it was. And it was true. Rather than get too caught up in how bitter those words tasted, he refocused on something that *was* his concern, the case.

"Here's the way I see this going down," he checked the time, "in twelve hours, give or take."

She sat straight up and then folded her arms over her chest.

"I go to the drop spot, which reminds me, I need to cancel the bank transaction," he said.

"They might be watching," she pointed out.

"So, you think it's best to go along as planned?"

"I'll give my full opinion once I've heard you out. So, keep going." There was a lot of reservation in her tone.

"I'm thinking that you need to be set up somewhere close but not where you'd be easily seen," he continued.

"And what about drones?"

"That's a big hole in my plan," he admitted. "One that I hope you can fill in for me."

She nodded, but he could almost see the reservations building up behind those beautiful eyes of hers.

"I continue on to the drop, as outlined by the perp or perps, whatever we're dealing with," he said. "With you nearby, I leave the spot and circle back. The perp's focus is going to be on getting the money and getting out of there."

"And we have no idea what tools he plans to use to do that. For instance, does he have ATVs nearby? Or a helicopter? A quarter of a million dollars isn't a drop in the bucket. I don't care who you are."

"No, it isn't," he agreed. But the amount wasn't as significant to a millionaire.

"What I mean by that is if the perp has been able to bilk this kind of money out of others, he's probably sitting on a fair chunk of change. Which means he could have a lot of resources to make sure he gets away with money in hand."

Coby agreed.

"Are you saying we'd be better off including more folks?" he asked.

"No. The more moving parts you have, the more opportunities you have of being discovered early and scaring off the perp. He'll be watching everything around him and be on high alert. If a deer so much as breaks a twig within ten feet of him, it's likely to be shot. He'll do the same for people too." She paused for a long moment and chewed on her thumbnail. "There are always a lot of unknowns in a situation like this. It's a big part of the reason federal agencies take months to build a case against major crime rings. Rushing the timeline is dangerous for all involved, and yet we all know the first forty-eight hours is critical in a kidnap-ping case."

"Are you saying I should just hand this over and hope for the best because I've never been good at handing over the reins," he warned.

"I understand that too. If this was a bigger operation, I'd have to insist we include law enforcement. Could I guar-antee no one would get hurt? No."

"Is there a baby involved? Tell me to the best of your ability based on your experience," he pleaded.

"The short answer is yes. But I have to warn you that she could be anyone's child, including the perp's," she said.

"What if she really belongs to Sarah? Looking back, there was something about her that made me feel sorry for her," he said.

"She might be an unwilling participant."

Coby didn't do helplessness, and yet that was exactly how he felt. Do nothing and he risked putting a mother and child in danger. Act and he risked putting himself and Laney in the hot zone. He wasn't as concerned about himself. He didn't doubt his ability to navigate himself out of a trick situation. It was the part about involving others he wasn't too keen on.

"What if I don't do anything? What if I walk away and pretend I never received the note? I could throw away the cell and focus on my own family," he said.

One of Laney's delicate eyebrows flew up. "Could you? I mean, it would force the perp's hand. Would you be able to walk away and not know the outcome?"

"With everything going on at the ranch, I think I could," he lied. He hated lying to her but it was the only way. If he told her his real plans, she'd insist on going with him. He couldn't risk her life and sleep at night if this thing went sour.

Besides, the perp was expecting him to come alone. Alone, he would be.

LANEY COULDN'T BELIEVE Coby's change of heart. Was it too good to be true?

"You should get some sleep," he said. There was something about the way he looked at her when he said it that told her sleep would be the last thing on her mind after this conversation.

"What about your case?" she asked.

"Forget it ever happened. You have it on good authority that Bobby Barrera is about to be blackmailed. You already know the perp's MO, so that should give you a head start," he said casually. It was like he'd flipped a switch and no longer cared. Was it too easy for him?

Because in the past twelve hours, she'd been with a man whose passion and honor code wouldn't let him walk away from a woman and child in distress.

"Are you sure you want to drop this?" she asked.

"One hundred percent." He spoke with confidence that made her believe him. Then, he added, "That pretty much wraps things up between us, so I'll just grab my stuff, then Diesel and I will get out of your hair."

What was up with the quick exit? This conversation felt off.

"It's late. You're welcome to crash on my couch," she offered, wanting him to stick around for more than just the case. If there was any chance she could get him to stay so she could work on him a little bit longer, she wouldn't hesitate.

"I've taken up too much of your time already." His words were spoken with finality. She'd lost and it was time to face the music. She also bit back a yawn, hoping the coffee would kick in soon. Her brain had the fog that came with a twenty-hour day. She was beyond tired and her second wind had yet to kick in. "Take your coffee to go, at least."

She pushed up to standing and located a travel mug. He was already up gathering his duffel and tucking everything inside. Then, he pocketed his own cell phone.

Diesel didn't so much as lift an eyelid.

"Okay then," he stood at the door like he couldn't get away from her fast enough. It shouldn't feel like rejection and she shouldn't let herself feel hurt by it even though that's exactly what she did on both counts.

He made kissing noises toward Diesel. The dog's head popped up. He looked around a little bit like he was trying to get his bearings. Then, he eased off the sofa and loped toward the back door.

It was probably just exhaustion that had Laney standing there, holding out a coffee mug, fighting back tears. She chalked it up to being near burnout already with her job but knew in her heart this was something so much more.

"Thank you." He took the cup and for a split second she saw something that looked a whole lot like regret in his eyes. But then, a man like him probably rarely second-guessed himself. It was probably just her *wanting* to see something there, *wishing* he was having a hard time walking out the door.

She took in a deep breath, pushed up to her tiptoes, and kissed him, needing to feel his lips move against hers one last time.

His muscles corded, and she thought he might just push her away. Instead, he opened his arms to let her move closer to him. She closed the distance between them and wrapped her arms around his neck.

It was difficult to think clearly with his strong male chest flush with hers. There was nothing more than a flimsy piece of cotton between them and she could feel every rock hard muscle. But then, she'd acted on impulse. Something she couldn't remember the last time she'd done.

Since she was the one who started this, it was her who needed to end it. Pulling on all her willpower, she did just that. Slowly.

He dropped the duffel on the floor and wrapped his arm around her waist to keep her from going too far. He rested his forehead on her and mumbled something about cursing his timing.

"Thank you for telling me about my father, by the way. It means a lot and I'm not sure I properly thanked you earlier." His deep timbre washed over her and through her.

"You're welcome. You needed to know." A tiny piece of her wished he asked if he could call her sometime. He didn't.

He just sucked in a burst of air like he was steeling his resolve, and then picked up his duffel. He whistled for Diesel to follow and she watched from the door as the pair disappeared into the darkness.

A single tear rolled down her cheek as an ache she'd never experienced before filled her chest. She fought against the tide trying to suck her under and hold her down.

She had a lot to think about and a plan to make.

14

Hours had passed since leaving Laney's house and the ache in Coby's chest had locked him up like a vise. Walking away from her had been one of the hardest things he'd ever done. But he had a mission he couldn't ignore, and he highly doubted she would ever want to talk to him again after. A hollow ache formed in his chest at the thought.

So, here it was dawn. He had a paper bag full of cash in his hand marked Feed and Seed. And he was whistling his way toward the drop spot in the meadow, questioning all his life choices up to this minute.

Making noise would ensure he didn't surprise anyone, especially the perp. If it was money the man wanted, it was money he would get.

Coby's plan being successful banked on a couple of assumptions. The first being he knew this area better than an outsider. The second, and this was a big one, he had a sneaky suspicion this guy was acting alone.

If he wasn't, Coby might be in more trouble than he

bargained for. That's why he brought his friends Smith & Wesson along. His M&P M2.0 fit snuggly in its holster. He had enough ammo to take care of a few folks should the need arise.

Diesel here would ensure no one got too close to him. Diesel was protective in the woods and he had a sixth sense about when Coby was uncomfortable in any situation. To say the animal would have Coby's back should anything go down was an understatement.

Making noise would also warn off any animals in the area that might get caught up in the skirmish as it went down.

Coby had zero intentions of allowing the perp to walk away with a bag of money. He had every intention of ensuring the guy served time for his crimes.

With Laney distracted and on the Bobby Barrera case that was unfolding, she was out of the way in case the worst happened. She would never forgive him for tricking her into thinking he wasn't going to act today. It was a sacrifice that had to be made despite the fact that she was the first person in longer than he could remember that he actually wanted to be around. Leaving her in the middle of the night had nearly shredded him.

There were some things he had to do alone. This was one of them. A part of him wanted to argue the opposite. She was the sheriff. She would know exactly what to do in a situation like this. She knew how to keep herself safe.

The rub in this situation was that he might have to do something illegal to catch this guy. Coby didn't want to be bound by laws. As a private citizen, he could take a shortcut if it presented itself to him.

Laney, on the other hand, was bound by rules and regulations. What had she called them? Protocols. Being good at her job meant something to her and there was no way she would take shortcuts. He respected her for it.

No matter how remote the chance, if a child's life was on the line, he wouldn't gamble. He would handle this himself. And then he would turn over the perp to the law.

Without a doubt, she would not want to speak to him when she realized what he'd done. He deserved it. A relationship had to be built on trust. Trust and communication. They had the second part down pat. And he trusted her with his life. She wouldn't trust him after this.

His chest squeezed so hard, taking in a breath hurt. And that was one of many reasons why he knew he'd been close to the real deal with her. Close to that same thing that had put silly grins on the faces of his brothers and cousins.

Coby had come straight to the meadow after leaving Laney's house last night. He'd worked long and hard, keeping busy until he'd heard the drone. She'd been right about it. Some of the more sophisticated poachers were using them now to survey a large area, using the information to make their next move.

He checked his cell phone. No activity.

The sun had disappeared behind the trees ten minutes ago, making it darker in the wooded area around the meadow. He'd refreshed his memory on this place. He'd studied the map until his eyes had crossed.

He was ready.

The perp's cell phone buzzed. He pulled it out.

R U here?

He responded with one word. *Yes.*

Money?

He sent the same response as before.

Did u brng frnds?

This time, Coby spelled out the two-letter word. *No.*

Hld for sec.

He'd been told where to go. The perp had already pushed the timeline back hours, ensuring it would be dark at the meetup. He brought the money. What was happening here? Of course, he couldn't anticipate everything but was the perp about to change the location? That was no good. All his preparation would be wasted at a new location. His stress response mounting, he kept moving toward the meadow, following the most likely path. He'd come at this from every angle in the past few hours, tracking which entry point the perp would expect him to take.

He mapped out the trajectory for the perp at every angle. He anticipated drones as much as possible. One operator would indicate one drone. He based all his assumptions on a lone wolf acting with a small network. Jackie looked all in, but what about Sarah? Was she in the scam of her own free will? He couldn't think of any decent person who would want to use their infant child to extort money from others.

Coby was certain the child was real, not a picture. He made an assumption the mother was real, and her name was Sarah.

As if to remind Coby of the stakes, the perp sent a video of a crying baby. The sound—so small and innocent—nearly cracked Coby's heart in two.

He tightened his grip on the cell, realizing his knuckles had gone sheet white.

All the more reason to stay the course. He was ready for the perp. The traps were set. A confrontation was unlikely, in Coby's estimation. His plan called for him being left instructions to drop the money and then leave. A drone would most likely appear around the edge of the meadow to ensure the drop had been made and then follow him out.

He'd already checked the trees and cleared them. No

cameras or recording devices of any kinds were found near the meadow. He'd been told by his cousin Levi that Laney had cracked the cold case of Ensley's brother's murder by looking up in the trees. Thinking about her hollowed out more of his chest. He was unsettled for a moment—a moment was all he could allow.

Unbeknownst to her, she'd been key to his plan. Standing in the woods hours ago, the story of how Laney had solved the mystery had come to mind. So, he'd stood in the center of the meadow and memorized the location of any tree that might afford a spying opportunity. There were six that had the best vantage points. He'd climbed each one to check for cameras.

After surveying every potential spying spot, he deduced the perp would most likely be using a drone. The guy wouldn't be stupid enough not to monitor the scene. Unless he was working with several others and brute force. Coby figured the perp would have requested more money if that were the case. Two hundred and fifty thousand dollars was a lot of money for one. Split it two or three ways and it didn't seem quite as substantial.

Mddle of the meadw. Drp + go. Now.

Coby took in a sharp breath. He was prepared for this if not ready. Not that his opinion mattered. He wasn't the one in charge and it was go time.

LANEY BLINKED HER EYES OPEN. The sun was almost down. She bit out a curse as she tried to shake the fog.

Oh, no. She'd fallen asleep.

That was so not good. She pushed up to standing and shook her head. She tapped her cheeks with the flat of her palms trying to get some blood flow going. She'd fallen asleep studying the map of the meadow.

A quick scan of what she was wearing said she needed to change out of the dress she had on. A glance at the clock said she didn't have time. So, she snatched her purse from off the counter, her holster from off the back of the sofa where she'd left it, and her car keys from the bowl near the front door.

She was out the door in two shakes with the nagging feeling she was going to be too late to talk reason into Coby.

Jumping into the department-issue vehicle, she flipped on her lights and then brought the engine to life. She gripped the steering wheel and mashed the gas pedal.

When she was five minutes out, she cut the lights and slowed her speed. Everything inside her wanted to be there already. Her pulse raced and her heart jackhammered the inside of her ribcage, pounding out a frantic rhythm.

Coby was going to try to be a hero. He'd shifted courses way too quickly and that had been her first red flag. The second, and this might just be a hope, was that he'd rejected her. She had to believe there was something special brewing between them. It was special to her and from every indication he felt the same way.

If she'd told him outright to stay home, he wouldn't have listened. Knowing him, the reason he'd left last night was so he wouldn't involve her in his plans. That also told her that he wasn't interested in doing things by the law.

Coby was exactly the kind of person who would put his life on the line for a stranger. It was one of his more admirable traits. At this point in time, it was also one of his most infuriating ones.

But she couldn't fault him for acting in a way he believed

was right. And she seriously couldn't fault him for wanting to do everything in his power to save a child.

So, he'd pushed her away last night.

Those were a lot of assumptions, and yet after getting to know him on a personal level, it was blindingly obvious to her that was exactly what he would do.

She brought the vehicle to a stop, tucked her purse underneath the driver's seat, and tucked keys in her pocket as she exited. Cell in one hand, weapon in the other, she surveyed the area before darting through the trees in a less worn path toward the meadow. She figured coming at it from the opposite side would catch people off guard. She also realized how dangerous the move was given the level of darkness and the fact that she would be surprising two people.

Branches slapped her face and chilly air whipped her hair around. She managed to pull a rubber band from her wrist and then secure her hair away from her face.

Coming in from this side of the meadow would take longer but it was her best shot at making it through undetected. The toe of her boot caught on underbrush and she face planted on the cold, unforgiving earth. Thankfully, she'd brought her elbows up in time to spare her face from actually smacking the ground. Not so lucky was her right elbow, which took a sharp stick. Her gun went tumbling out of her hand so she immediately scrambled up on all fours to feel around for it.

She dimmed the light on her cell to next to nothing before turning on the flashlight app. She kept it low to the ground and found her gun. Issuing a sigh of relief, she sat up. There was no time to inspect her injuries, only to regroup.

Scrambling to her feet, she brushed off debris and

pushed ahead. The small light kept her from making the same mistake twice. Plus, she had to move at a slower pace as the trees thickened. Winding in and around the trunks, she raced as quickly as she could.

It occurred to her that she might be lost. It would be so easy to get turned around in the thicket. Kicking through scrub brush that was a foot high, she kept pushing until her thighs hurt and her lungs burned.

She should be there by now.

Laney bit out a curse. *No. No. No.* This couldn't be happening. Not when Coby could be in serious danger.

A couple of deep breaths later, and she checked her cell for coverage. Zero bars, so that wasn't exactly reassuring. No cell coverage meant no calling for backup in an emergency. Frustrated with herself, she resumed the search for the meadow.

She'd memorized the markers in the daytime. It was easy to get turned around at night, despite coming here once or twice a week just to check on the former crime scene. Grim locations like this one could prove popular with teenagers and she saw it as her job to make sure no one else met the same fate as two pre-teen boys had a decade ago.

Laney shivered against the cold, realizing in her hasty exit from home that she'd forgotten her jacket. The white minidress was no match against the frigid air. She knew better. It was her own fault if she ended up with exposure.

She stopped. Running around in circles would be fruitless and she was pretty certain she'd seen the same boulder ten minutes ago.

Glancing around, she tried to get her bearings. Which way to go? Without her map to navigate by, she might as well admit to being lost. Could she even circle back and find her way out of the woods at this point?

There was silence except for the sounds of insects chirping. Another cold shiver raced down her spine. She hated insects. She hated being in the meadow at night. This was the same place she'd investigated a gruesome murder of innocent preteens. Even though the act had been committed a decade ago, it felt like yesterday as the images stamped her thoughts. Images of blood and devastation. An involuntary shiver rocked her body. She got the feeling people referred to when they said a cat walked over their grave.

A crack of a bullet shattered the quiet.

Laney spun to her left and bolted toward the sound.

15

Coby dropped to the dirt onto all fours. Using his heft, he physically blocked Diesel from the possibility of bullet fragments.

When he was certain it was safe to move, he crawled behind a thick tree stump, urging Diesel to follow. He did but he quickly turned his attention toward the direction of the bullet from a moment ago.

He couldn't be certain the shooter knew his location until another bullet cracked, and then pinged off the tree behind him. The aim was a little too high and a little to the right. Or he would have taken a bullet to the brain.

The whir of a flying object overhead caught his attention. Drone. He felt around on the ground for a weapon as Diesel locked in on the noise and started rapid-fire barking. The person behind the controls would definitely be able to locate them if Diesel continued.

"Hey, be cool, buddy." Coby needed something substantial to be able to chunk at the darn thing. He had a few choice words for it, but they wouldn't be very threatening to a machine.

His fingers connected with a sharp edge. He felt around and then palmed the softball-sized rock. He could only hope that all those years on the baseball diamond pitching games in the backyard was about to pay off.

Coby hopped up onto his knees, drew back his right hand as he took aim, and then launched the rock toward the whirring noise. A clunk sound said he made contact and a glint of metal careening toward the earth said he nailed the target. His cousin Ryan, the former star baseball player, would be proud right now.

But he didn't wait to see if the thing was damaged behind repair. Instead, he followed it to the ground and then grabbed whatever he could find as he scrambled over toward it. In this case, it was a stick. As he neared, the drone tried to lift itself off the ground.

Coby stomped the heel of this boot on it, grinding it into the earth. He tossed the stick aside and made darn sure the drone was toast before urging Diesel to follow. Enough damage had been done and the perp had a general idea where to look for them. Not good.

It was getting dark and, therefore, harder to see much more than a few feet in front of him. Diesel was on full alert and he was moving with a slight limp on his left hindquarter.

Coby smoothed his hand along the dog's back and leg. Diesel drew his leg up the minute Coby felt liquid. He brought his hand around and saw blood. Not gushing, not a lot. But it was concerning all the same.

Using his flashlight app, he risked a closer look.

A wild bullet flew past his head within a couple of inches, so he abandoned his plan in favor of getting them to safety first. Then, he could deal with the injury. White-hot anger licked through his veins at the thought of Diesel being grazed by a bullet.

"Let's go," he urged, taking the lead. Diesel would follow without question. He was loyal to a fault.

The thought of Coby being responsible for Diesel's injury was a gut punch. The very first person he wanted to talk to the minute this was all over and Diesel was safe, was Laney. He surprised himself in how much he missed her. It was like someone cut him in half, which was a strange feeling at best because he'd always prided himself on his independence, never needing anyone.

Moving quickly through the dense trees, he effectively circled the meadow. He'd made the drop and been given orders to leave. There were two spots in the meadow where cell coverage was possible. One bar, but coverage nonetheless. Now, he'd moved away from one of them. He was making a circle around the meadow.

Now, it was a game of Red Rover.

He'd laid down the gauntlet by making the drop. He wasn't about to leave the area. If the perp wanted the money, it was his turn to take a risk. He had, after all, been the one to orchestrate this little game. Time to ante up.

Coby stopped, crouched down low, and listened.

A noise to his far left, shifted his attention. It could be a ploy. The perp could have set up a decoy. It was exactly the type of thing Coby would do, so he took off to the right. Diesel followed, keeping pace. The pair of them weren't exactly quiet as they moved. Coby located another rock and tossed it in the general direction of the noise, hoping to throw the perp off track.

He also figured his assumption there was only one perp was dead on as he hooked another left, moving as quietly as possible. The urge to get Diesel out of there and check on his wound was hard to suppress.

The perp would make a move for the money soon and Coby would be right on him. Another sound, this time closer, surprised him. It was coming from the opposite side. His theory about one perp must be wrong.

Coby crouched down low, putting his hand out to stop Diesel without giving a verbal command. *Come on.*

And then he heard what he'd been hoping for. The yelp of someone being caught off guard and in a trap. Coby smiled. *Gotcha.*

One of his traps was twenty-five feet away, give or take. The others were farther and, based on the direction and volume of the yelp, the closest one had snared someone. He'd spent the day digging, and it looked like it was going to pay off big time. This fell into the category of time well spent.

The perp could easily still have a weapon, so Coby had to be careful in his approach. He wouldn't take anything for granted with this guy. In the same vein, as much as his heart was breaking that he couldn't stop to check Diesel, Coby couldn't waver until the perp subdued, knocked out, tied up, or both. He didn't care so long as the guy couldn't hurt anyone else.

As he neared, his pulse kicked up a couple of notches. He heard grunting and struggling and it wasn't coming from the person he wanted it to be. As he neared the mouth of the trap, he said, "Laney?"

"Coby. Get me out of here." The fear in her voice was a gut punch. He also knew he couldn't help her right away. Not until he made certain the perp hadn't followed him.

"Hold tight." He circled the perimeter, giving a wide berth to the ten foot hole he'd dug. The recent rain would make it impossible to get a good grip and the hole was wide enough that no one would be able to plant their hands and feet on opposite sides and climb up.

He'd covered it with branches and leaves. His plan had been to lead the perp to one of the holes where he would fall in. Coby hadn't banked on Laney following, no matter how much his heart swelled that he was going to see her again—when he was certain he hadn't been followed.

Moving as quickly as he could without drawing more unwanted attention, he cleared the area and then dropped down next to the hole. He took off his belt and dropped it down. "Do you have your phone?"

"Yes." The sound of her voice broke through what was left of the casing that he'd built around his heart.

"Shine it up so you can see the belt," he whispered.

She did, and then a second later, she grabbed onto the strap. The light disappeared as she climbed up the wall. When she got close enough to the top. He dropped his hand down. She grabbed on and, with some effort, he managed to pull her out of the hole at the same time he heard Diesel's low-pitched growl.

"I'll go for him. You roll out of sight."

Laney didn't have time to argue with Coby. Lost seconds could mean the difference between life and death for them both and she wouldn't risk losing him again.

So, she rolled out of sight and behind a nearby tree. She kept her ear to the ground to make certain the perp wouldn't come up from behind them. At this point, the perp had to know he wasn't getting out of the woods unscathed if Coby had anything to say about it.

A guy with nothing to lose wasn't a good person to have on their tail. Thankfully, when she'd fallen into the trap, her gun had come down with her. The safety had been on and that had stopped her from firing while going down.

At least she had that going for her. She'd taken a hard landing on her right side and would have a couple of choice bruises tomorrow to prove it. But she was all right. Better yet, she was out of there. And Diesel's barks said the perp was getting closer.

Laney slowed her breathing, closed her eyes, and listened. Diesel was going after it at this point, giving away their location. Coby seemed resigned to the fact his dog wouldn't stop and he made no effort to quiet him. At least, none that she could hear. And, besides, it most likely wouldn't do any good anyway.

Her right ankle screamed at her when she put weight on it, so that was a disadvantage she needed to take into consideration. She was a great shot if she could see, but night had descended all around them and they were immersed in pitch black at this point.

Turning on her phone app was akin to placing a target on her forehead, so that was a no-go. She would just have to fumble her way through the dark, and hope for a clean takedown or shot if he proved a threat.

She'd already heard a shot but hearing and seeing were two different things and law enforcement had a strict line to tow, as it should be when faced with taking someone's life.

Laney twisted right when she heard a noise from behind her. She bit out a curse. Say something to Coby and she risked giving away her own location. Take away the element of surprise and she might as well shine a flashlight on herself, step out with her arms in the air, and call for a surrender.

And then she heard what no one wanted to in this situation, an infant cry.

She eased around the tree trunk as the footsteps neared. Her eyes were beginning to adjust to the darkness but just barely. She needed more time but wasn't going to get it.

Back against the tree, she prayed the perp didn't spot her as he walked past with what she could now see was a mother and child. He had a gun to the mother's head.

"I'll kill them both if you don't call off that damn dog," the perp shouted. He was average height and build, which in Texas meant close to six-feet-tall. He couldn't be a day over thirty-five. She guessed around thirty-two to thirty-three years old.

The woman, Laney presumed, was Sarah.

"I told him that she isn't yours," she said through tears.

"She's a liar," the perp's voice sounded agitated. Not good. His heightened emotions could make him trigger happy.

"Hold on there a minute," Coby's voice boomed. Diesel's low growl a threat not to get any closer.

The perp stopped ten feet away from the tree where Laney stood. He'd walked right past, too focused on Coby and Diesel to notice her.

"You can drop your weapon," the perp said to Coby.

It was now or never.

"This is Sheriff Justice. Put your hands where I can see 'em or I'll shoot." She came around the back of the tree, using it as cover, and by sheer force of will stood on both feet without grimacing.

"Wait. What?" The perp turned his head. He looked from her to Coby and back.

"Hands where I can see 'em. Now," she demanded.

Coby had the good sense to take cover as well. She also noticed that he'd put the hole in between him and the perp.

"I'll shoot him if you don't put your gun away," the perp said before checking to make certain that was an option.

"Do not force me to use deadly force, sir. Now, put your weapon down and your hands up."

He spun around, forcing mother and child to act as a human shield against her. Coby couldn't shoot from the back without possibly fatally injuring them as well.

The first break came when he started backing away from her. He seemed to think Coby was his best option.

"You're surrounded, sir. For the third time, put down your weapon and keep your hands where I can see them." She used her authoritative sheriff tone.

A few more steps and he would fall into the hole. Would he drag mother and infant down with him?

"Stop where you are..." The command came out too late, his heel dropped, his ankle twisted, and his arms went out wide. A wild shot fired as the gun flew from his hand.

Laney bolted toward the victims, grabbing hold of Sarah's shirt. They both started down, but Laney twisted and reached for the baby. She landed hard on the same right side that was still angry from earlier but the infant was spared hitting the ground. The little girl's mother dove over Laney, hitting the ground hard and rolling.

Coby was by Laney's side in a heartbeat, helping her sit up. He shined a light onto the perp in the hole and relief flooded her that no other weapons were visible. The perp was flat on his back, the wind clearly knocked out of him.

And then Sarah rolled over, gun in hand. She must've located the perp's weapon.

"Give her back to me right now," she demanded, her voice shaky.

"She's okay. You're okay," Laney soothed. In an attempt to save mother and baby, she'd dropped her gun. "Just take in a breath and ask yourself if you really want to do this right now."

"I want my baby," there was so much desperation in her voice now.

"And she's right here," Laney soothed. Was Sarah in shock?

"He made me do it." She brought her free hand up to her face and cried.

"Set the gun down so we can get you the help you need." Laney knew better than to make promises she couldn't keep. Help didn't necessarily mean Sarah wouldn't do the time for her part if she'd been a willing participant. Not to mention the fact it was never okay to pull a gun on an officer of the law.

Sarah tossed the gun like she suddenly realized she was holding something lethal. A shot fired as the weapon hit the ground.

Laney gasped as the white-hot pain of scorching metal slammed into her hip.

"Hold on tight. I'm going for help," Coby said before taking off.

Within twenty minutes, the woods were teaming with emergency personnel. Sarah held her baby tight in her arms while Laney stemmed the bleeding on her hip. It wasn't nearly as bad as it had felt in the moment.

Thankfully, the bullet grazed her rather than embedded. On balance, she'd been incredibly lucky. She looked at Coby, who was working on Diesel's scrapes, and saw home.

Did he feel the same?

16

"I thought I was going to lose you." Coby looped his hands around Laney's waist as the last of the emergency workers cleared the scene. He was careful not to touch the bandage on her hip.

"I'm here, Coby. Right where I want to be." Those words were music to his ears.

The perp, Sawyer Easton, confessed to forcing women with infants to claim celebrity men had fathered their child. He preyed on those who needed money and didn't tell them what they were really getting into until it was too late.

Shame was the cover for his crimes. The men were ashamed to let the baby news go public. The women were ashamed they'd been recruited to hurt someone else.

Sarah wasn't getting off scot-free but hers was a lesser crime and she was also a victim. In exchange for her testimony, they would most likely be able to work out a deal so that she wouldn't be separated from her baby.

"How did you know that I would come here?" he asked Laney.

"You're not that hard to read if someone knows the kind of person you are. There was no way your compassion would allow someone else to suffer if you had the power to change it." She was right. She had him pegged. "And I love that about you."

He started to ask his next question but stalled out for a second. "Hold on. Do you mean it?"

She looked at him like he had three chins.

"You said you 'love' that about me. What exactly does that word cover?"

Those beautiful cheeks of hers turned crimson again. "I love you, Coby." She threw her hands up in the air. "I've got nothing to hide. As crazy as this is going to sound, I fell head over heels for you in the space of half a day. How's that for crazy?"

"I have a better word. Spontaneous." He couldn't contain his smile. It was ear-to-ear. "You have no idea how relieved I am to hear you say that, Laney Justice."

"Relieved?" she asked.

"Well, I didn't want to be the first to cop to it. But falling in love with you doesn't sound crazy to me at all," he admitted.

"No?" She cocked an eyebrow, and all he could think about was how close he'd come to losing her.

"We're not twenty-year-old kids who have no idea what they want in life. We're experienced adults. We've been with enough people to know when a good thing comes along. Don't you think?" he asked.

She pushed up to her tiptoes and kissed him. "I don't think. I know. The minute we talked one-on-one, I realized there was something special about you. I'd hoped there could be something special between us. Something that could last. My rational mind tried to talk me out of it, but my heart wouldn't listen. If someone had told me this was a possibility, I would never have believed them. I'm crazy about you and it's the most logical thing to me now."

"Good. Because I'm crazy about you right back." He feathered kisses on her chin, then on the tip of her nose. "And I don't want this to end."

"Does it have to?" she asked. "Because I know exactly what I want, Coby. And I'm talking about for the rest of my life. I never wanted to take a break from work until I met you. I never thought about days off until I met you. I never thought anything could mean more to me than..."

He liked where this was going, so the fact that she stopped cold was ever more jarring.

"But, wait," she said. Two words he never wanted to hear at a time like this. "There's something about me. I told you about it before. It's not fair to ask you to give up having a family of your own because I can't—"

"Can't what?" He cut in. He had an idea where this was going and she needed to know exactly how he felt about it.

"Have children," she said.

"Says who?" he asked.

"My doctor and—"

"Your doctor said you can't carry children. There's a difference," he pointed out. She needed to know that wasn't a game-changer for him.

"Yes, there is but, Coby, don't deny that you want your own children." She looked him straight in the eye, daring him.

"I won't deny that I'd like to have a family someday. But there's a caveat. I want a family with *you*."

"But I can't—"

"Yes, you can." He brought his hand up to her face and brushed an errant strand of hair out of her eyelash. "The only thing that matters to me is that you *want* kids. How we get them or whose DNA they have won't make them less ours."

"You say that now," she started to argue.

"But what? I love Diesel more than words can express and we don't share a strand of genetic material. Doesn't stop me from thinking he's my kid."

She looked over his shoulder like she did when she was seriously contemplating something.

"We don't have to rush, if you're not sure about us. We can take it slow if you want. Understand that I'd be doing it for you, though. I know exactly what I want. You, me, and Diesel are all the family I need. If kids came along through us or adoption, I see that as the cherry on top." And since he wanted her to know just how dead serious he was, he dropped down on one knee right there in the meadow. "Laney Justice, I have never wanted to stay up all night and talk to anyone as much as I want to with you. I never experienced the kind of relationship that completes me in a way I never knew anything was missing. I'm whole without you but I'm so much better than that with you."

She brought her hands up to her face and sucked in a breath as tears streamed down her cheeks.

"I know I've found the person I'm supposed to be with for the rest of my life. Now, it's up to you to decide if you feel the same way." He took her hand in his. "I'd be the happiest man on the planet and beyond if you would consider marrying me."

He started to tell her that she didn't have to decide anything right then, but he was quieted by a head nod.

"Yes, Coby. I think I fell in love with you the minute we spent time alone together. There was something different about every minute I spent with you. I can't imagine being with anyone else and if you can accept me as I am, I would absolutely marry you."

"Something smells good." Coby entered the kitchen after lining up his boots in back, along with the others. The low hum of conversation could be heard from the doorway.

Levi and Ensley stood closest to the door. His eldest cousin pulled him into a bear hug the minute he turned around. Coby hugged his newly minted cousin-in-law next before his gaze cut across the room to Laney, who was leaning against the wall near the dining table, chatting easily with Ryan and Alexis.

Laney's relaxed posture calmed his nerves. He wanted her to get along with his family. More than that, he wanted her to feel comfortable around them. She'd been instrumental in solving quite a few crimes affecting the family in recent months. Everyone seemed just as comfortable around her, save for one person. Donny.

Uncle Clive looked to be gaining some of his strength back after his fight to come back after being in a coma. His color had returned and he looked less like a shell of a man. His arms were starting to fill out again.

A.J. and Tess sat opposite Kurt and Arianna. Paisley cooed in her stepmother's lap. Declan and Piper were at the table, along with her grandmother. Jack and Natalie were engaged in deep conversation with Dalton and Brielle, who looked enraptured with whatever was being said. Then there was Coby's brother Reed along with Addison. They were laughing at something Hayden and Mika were saying.

The house was lively and full despite the absence of two of Coby's brothers. If he'd learned anything in the past few days, it was that happiness was fleeting. When it came, no matter what form it took, all anyone could do was grab hold and hang on for the ride. If taco trucks gave two of his brothers the kind of happiness they deserved, far be it from him to say they were wrong for leaving the family business.

He would miss them, though.

Miss Penny stood at the kitchen sink, Hawk by her side as she washed a glass. When she handed the glass to Hawk for him to place inside the dishwasher, Coby caught sight of something sparkling on a particular finger. He elbowed Levi and nodded toward the couple.

"I know," Levi whispered.

"Isn't it adorable," Ensley beamed.

"As a matter of fact, it kind of is," he agreed. "And about time."

Uncle Clive stood up and called for attention as Coby excused himself. Being away from Laney caused a physical ache and he wanted to be near her while announcements were made.

He made it over in time for the voices around the room to hush. He kissed Laney and the voices didn't stay quiet for long. They whooped and hollered. There were a couple of whistles and cheers.

Coby waved a dismissive hand at the small crowd.

"Thank you all for coming to dinner tonight," Uncle Clive began. "You can't begin to know how much it means to me to have most of the family under one roof again."

There were a few nods of appreciation.

"I won't talk long. It'd be a sin to let food get cold and it's getting close to done, but Hawk has an important announcement and then I'll say a few words before we eat if that's agreeable to everyone in the room."

More of those nods came.

"Then, I'll hand over the announcements to Hawk," Uncle Clive said. He looked over at his longtime foreman, whose grin was ear-to-ear.

"I think most of you have been speculating what could be going on between myself and this beautiful lady." He motioned toward Miss Penny, whose cheeks turned six shades past red. She wasn't one for being in the spotlight. "Last night, I asked if she would do me the incredible honor of marrying me. And she made me the luckiest man in the world when she said yes."

If the hooting and hollering for Coby's kiss was loud, the excitement that followed Hawk's announcement was out of this world. Fists pounded against the table in unison as a chorus of congratulations rang out. Each took a turn hugging Miss Penny and Hawk.

Uncle Clive moved to the fridge and started handing out champagne bottles. Glasses were poured and a toast to posterity was made.

Miss Penny deserved all the happiness in the world. Coby thought about the word happiness. It seemed to be his theme today. Not that he was complaining as he looked across the room at a family that had seemed to be standing on opposite shores too long.

When the glasses slowly stopped clanking and the

cheers slowed, Uncle Clive once again stood at the head of the table. "As you all know, we've been through a rough patch. One, I think every single one of us worried at some point or another we wouldn't get past."

The room became quiet enough to hear a pin drop.

"My brother has a few words to speak." With that, Uncle Clive turned the floor over.

Donny stood up and took a step back before thanking Uncle Clive. "My brother has been kind enough to listen to me in private, and I'd like for all of you to hear what I'm about to say from the horse's mouth, so to speak. If I may."

Slowly, heads nodded.

"First, I want to say that I appreciate each and every one of you for your patience with me. In jail, I had a lot of time to think about my life, my choices." He didn't meet anyone's gaze when he paused for a few seconds before continuing, "I haven't lived my life in the best way. I realize that. My coming home has caused a lot of stress for all of you, and I apologize for that. I also want to say that I'm grateful to my brother for always believing the best in me, even when I did nothing to deserve it."

Uncle Clive put a hand on Donny's shoulder in a show of support.

"To my nephews, you were right to be suspicious of me. I did come back thinking I was owed something." Again, he studied the floor like it was the MCat and he was trying to get into medical school. "I want you all to know that I've had legal papers drawn up and signed stating that I will never ask for nor should I inherit any of the family ranch. I don't deserve it and should never had tried to go behind my brother's back to get a share. I violated everyone's trust in the room, and for that, I'm truly sorry."

Everyone seemed to be processing the statements.

"To my sons..." Donny's voice cracked. He seemed to need a few seconds to gather himself before he continued, "I realize I don't have a right to call you that. I haven't been the father you needed or deserved. I stepped aside to allow my brother to raise you when I was afraid I'd screw it up. I was never good enough, never what you deserved. And I realize that I'd be asking way too much of you to ask for forgiveness, so I won't."

More of that quiet filled the room for a few more seconds.

"I would like a chance to be part of your lives. To get to know the men you've become. Men, who I aspire to be like someday." His voice hitched again. "I can't undo the past—"

"No one can," Uncle Clive was quick to come to Donny's defense.

When Coby really looked at his uncle, he could see the moisture forming in his eyes.

"I'm learning to take life one step at a time. And if you'll give me the chance to prove myself again, it would mean the world," Donny continued with a shaky voice. "And if you can't, I'll have no hard feelings."

Coby wondered about second chances. His father had burned through a lot of trust. But if he was sincere, Coby could take a step forward.

"I've moved my things into the bunkhouse and am grateful to my brother for a place to stay," Donny continued.

"You don't have to do that," Uncle Clive said.

"Yes, I do," Donny defended.

Donny had a lot to prove before he could gain back Coby's trust. Based on the look on the faces around the room, Coby wasn't alone.

It was probably all this happiness talking, but a second

chance sounded good to him. He stood up, walked over to Donny, and brought him into a hug.

"You have a lot of work to do to restore trust," Coby said to his father. "But I'm willing to give it a shot."

A couple of tears tumbled down Donny's cheeks as Coby stepped aside and the others followed suit. When the last hug was doled out, Uncle Clive said the two words everyone was ready to hear.

"Let's eat."

BONUS CHAPTER FROM TEXAS COWBOY'S PROTECTION

Regina Anderson tucked her earbuds in, tied off her running shoes, and pushed off her front porch. She turned up the volume on the heavy metal rock band music she played. Mornings sucked. Running sucked. Loud music sucked. The ritual kept Gina, as everyone but her mother called her, from taking her anger out on the world.

The loose, wet gravel on the drive of the fishing cabin caused her foot to slip as she rounded the corner onto the familiar country road. A couple extra forward steps righted her as she struggled to find her pace. Those first few steps were always the hardest to take, she reminded herself. Nothing in her wanted to do this.

The morning air didn't help matters. With every breath, she felt the crisp edge to the frigid temperature burning her lungs. The simple act of taking in oxygen was the equivalent to painful stabs at her rib cage.

Gina pounded the pavement with her feet. The stress of a major move with a baby, even though she was moving back to the small town where she'd grown up, had given her a tension headache.

It was early. Six a.m. was an ungodly hour.

Head throbbing, what she really wanted was caffeine. Big cup. Quiet room. The quiet room was a fantasy once her daughter, Everly, woke but the coffee was realistic.

The sun beat down on a spot at the crown of Gina's head. April weather in Gunner, Texas, was unpredictable. Today, the sun was out and the temperature was expected to hover around forty-seven degrees. This time of year, days could be swallowed up with thunderstorms and the kind of lightning that raced sideways for miles across a dark sky. Much like the thunderstorm from last night, but Gina didn't mind. That kind of weather matched her mood.

At thirty-two-years-old, she was a single mom to a little girl who would never know her father, a man who'd been so anxious for his daughter's arrival he'd painted her room pink the day a sonogram revealed her sex. Little did Gina know it would be the last day she'd ever see her husband again. Their daughter, Everly, would never meet her father.

The music matched the level of her anger at losing a decent man who would've been a great father. The things she would go back and do differently if she could. The regret that filled her chest and hardened her heart toward the world, but not towards Everly, was heavier today.

Bright sunny days just soured her. The run gave her a sense of normalcy in a world that had turned upside down. She'd stayed in Dallas for the rest of her pregnancy; bringing her baby home to the house she'd shared with Des had been important to her. After all the work he'd done on the nursery, she wanted baby Everly to spend her first year there. It only seemed right to Gina, a small way to honor Des.

Gina's mother had put up a strong argument for her to move home to Gunner so she would have help with the baby. Gina loved her mother, don't get her wrong; the woman was a saint in many ways. But she just hadn't been ready to love her mother full-time. Mom was a little too free with advice about pretty much every aspect of life and a little too needy when it came to attention.

Growing up, it had only been Gina and her parents. There'd been no siblings or cousins around, no extended family. Gina had always wondered what it would be like to be surrounded by a large family. Big holiday gatherings with all the trimmings. Boisterous laughter around a table brimming with every food a kid could imagine. Kids running around wild and happy. Her parents had been busy with the restaurant, or too tired from it to do anything but relax after work, and so she'd been left to her own devices for much of her childhood.

Mom had been right about one thing, though. Everly needed as much family to surround her as possible, even if it was down to an overbearing mother and her friends.

Thinking about the piles of unopened boxes lining the walls of the family's cabin on the lake, Gina already felt defeated. She would get there, she reminded herself on almost an hourly basis. It had become her mantra.

The boxes would eventually be unpacked. She'd make the two-bedroom cabin feel like home. It might take some time, especially considering she had a little one to care for and was starting right in with the family restaurant tomorrow, but the work would get done. It always did.

It was good to remind herself of her other favorite mantra in moments like these. *Chin up. Smile on. Power through.* God, she was so damn tired from 'powering through' the past year-and-a-half.

Plus, she'd always planned to come back and take over the family business at some point. It's what her mother had done. And her grandmother before that. The restaurant had been operating in Gunner for three generations already. Gina would be number four and she hoped Everly would want to carry on the tradition someday. But only if she wanted to. Gina wouldn't force her daughter into a life she didn't want.

For Gina, the restaurant gave her a connection to family. There was so little of that left. Another benefit now that she was a single mother came in the form of extra time with her daughter. A breakfast-only job would make Gina more available to Everly and after losing Des so suddenly, she was never more aware of just how precious time could be.

Those thoughts were too heavy for this early in the morning. She cranked up the volume but even the loud drum banging and screech of a metal guitar couldn't distract her today. She hated days like this where missing Des was an ache. There were too many days she didn't want to get out of bed. In times like these she felt the dark clouds hanging over her head might never clear.

The sun comes out in every season, even spring. How many times had her mother repeated the mantra? It obviously gave her mother great comfort. For Gina, not so much. The only bright spot in Gina's past year was asleep in a crib while her new babysitter hovered.

Gina rounded the corner onto a country road and finally hit her stride. At least her run was working for her this morning. The runner's high kicked in, temporarily abating her need for a caffeine IV, although she wouldn't turn one down. The move had brought on plenty of additional stress. Then there was leaving her job—a job that had been her lifeline in recent months.

The heavy metal band, RockSlam, pounded her ears, penetrating her thoughts, numbing her. A half hour into her run and it had finally hit. This was the point that made the whole get-out-of-bed early bit worth it. The point when she took control of her thoughts and could bury the heartbreak. The moment when she believed she'd actually be able to get through the day and maybe somehow be okay.

Her thighs no longer burned and her head stopped hurting for a few glorious minutes that, when she was lucky, turned into hours. It wasn't exactly peace, but her brain was still. And that was the best she could hope for under the circumstances.

Rounding the next bend, she was in top form. She let go of the belief she was crazy for forcing herself out of bed. She let go of all the thoughts that constantly churned in her head. She just let go.

And then something hit her, knocking her out of her rhythm. An awful smell blasted her nostrils. At the rate she was breathing, it hit hard. She coughed hard enough to break her stride.

The acrid smell could only come from a dead animal. Out at the lake, that wasn't uncommon. Whatever it was, it must've been dead for hours or days. Gina pulled the collar of her cotton T-shirt up and over to cover her nose and mouth. A few more steps in and her gag reflex engaged.

A side cramp stopped her, doubling her over. She took her earbuds out and glanced around, searching for the cause of the stench. She could make a call to animal control if she could figure out where the smell came from.

Checking underbrush, she heard a sound—like a dog whimpering—to her left. She steeled herself for what she might find and headed toward the noise.

Yesterday's rain had everything soaked. Her running

shoes were swamped with mud as she pushed closer to the wounded animal. And then she saw something move under a scrub bush. As she got closer, she saw a black Labrador retriever on his side.

Gina made slow and deliberate movements toward the animal. "You're okay, buddy."

The dog cried as he rolled onto his belly and tried to crawl toward her. She could see his tail wagging. He was friendly. Someone's pet?

Gina had only moved in two days ago. She hadn't had five minutes to introduce herself to the neighbors. Being on acre lots made privacy even easier and that was part of the reason she'd taken over the family cabin. That, and the fact rent was affordable. The restaurant did okay, but there was just enough money to set her mother up with retirement and give Gina enough of a salary to raise her daughter.

"You're a good boy." Gina bent down, making herself as small as possible so the dog wouldn't see her as a threat. He hadn't give her any indication that he would bite. At least not so far. Still, a wounded animal could be unpredictable.

Labradors were great dogs, though, and he seemed to know on instinct she was there to help. He moved again and that's when she saw the blood. A lot of it. Gina moved to his side and smoothed her hand along his body.

And then she found it. Bullet hole. Who in God's name would hurt such a beautiful animal? And how could she live right down the street and not hear it? The storm. Thunder pounded last night. It must've muffled the noise. "Hold on, buddy. We'll get some help." Anger raged through her as she pulled out her cell.

Gina took off the jacket tied around her waist and put pressure on the spot where the animal bled. Her first call was to her mother. The woman had half the town on speed dial. She knew everyone. Gina quickly explained where she was and what she'd found. The second call was to her babysitter to let her know she'd be running late.

The dog stirred. He was trying to get up.

Stroking the animal's fur, tears blinded her. Who could be so cruel?

And then it dawned on her. The acrid smell. It wasn't coming from the animal. She cursed.

He kept trying to get up. Was he trying to take her to his master?

From out of nowhere, Gina heard a twig snap right behind her. She made a move to whirl around. The strike to the back of her head barely registered. Everything went black.

GINA BLINKED BLURRY EYES OPEN. Her head pounded and she felt an overwhelming urge to vomit. Her stomach roiled as she bounced up and down. Panic gripped her. Her first thought was Everly. If something happened to Gina, what would happen to her daughter?

Moving was next to impossible. She struggled to gain her bearings. It didn't take long for her to figure out she was in the back of a vehicle. Some kind of SUV. The driver was speeding, too. A getaway?

Her wrists hurt and so did her ankles. She was bound in some way. The cold metal cutting into her wrists gave her the answer. *Cuffs.*

The dog. Her heart ached for the Labrador she'd been trying to save. Was he just left there to die? That poor animal. A sob escaped against the tape covering her mouth. Gina stuffed her panic down deep. Call it survival instinct.

She'd gotten good at denying her emotions in the last eighteen months. Hell, she could go further back than that, but Des was gone. She was a widow. There was no use thinking about the shortcomings in their marriage now.

Right now, all she cared about was getting home to Everly. Determination welled inside her as she took a mental inventory. Hands tied behind her back. On her side. She maneuvered, slipping her hands around her legs and in front of her without drawing attention.

Then she paused, listening for any clues about who was in the vehicle with her. From what she could discern, there was only one person in the car. She didn't want to think about what that meant for the Labrador who'd been left all alone. She *couldn't* think about that right now if she wanted to live. And she needed to live.

Was there anything inside the vehicle she could use as a weapon?

Gina tried to twist out of the metal cuffs. They were generic, the kind anyone could buy off the internet so she doubted the man driving was in law enforcement. She managed to squeeze the left cuff off her wrist and then the right. Her hands immediately flew to her ankles.

No such luck there. Those weren't coming off so easily.

At least her hands were free. She had no idea how long she'd been out of it. The sun was still rising, so she couldn't have been out for long. She flattened her palm on the floorboard and felt around. There had to be something she could use against her assailant.

Cell phone.

She felt around in her pockets and then remembered she'd had it out after calling her mother. Since it wasn't on her person, she figured it was probably back in the mud.

Bouncing around, she did her best not to make a peep.

Her skull felt like it had been cracked open. She felt around and winced when her fingers landed on a lump the size of a golf ball.

Where was she? In town? She'd only been back in Gunner for two nights but she'd grown up here and visited often. There wasn't much about the area that could throw her for a loop. Could she risk a glance without giving herself away?

The main thing she had going for her right now was that the driver had no idea she was awake and alert.

The SUV slowed to a stop. A stop sign? A red light?

With her hands in front of her and the cuffs off, she could open the emergency hatch. She'd read somewhere a long time ago that if someone was abducting her to make the biggest racket as fast as she could. Lying low was a bad idea. If the person got her to a different location it would be secure and would drastically cut her chances of survival or escape.

The thought of being stuck in a home or building with no escape, no chance to see her daughter hit Gina hard. This was not happening. This could not happen. Everly was not losing both of her parents.

Determination fueled her next bold move. She popped up, saw the dark-eyed man's gaze grow wild in the rearview mirror. She pulled the trunk latch and the door opened. A beeping sound alerted the driver. He already knew.

Those dark eyes of his burned into her memory as his gaze bore into her. He turned his head to one side and she caught the outline of his profile through the ski mask. She focused on details. Hooked nose. Long chin. Tall forehead.

He stomped the gas pedal. She tucked and rolled out the SUV.

The hard concrete pounded her shoulder. She tucked

her chin to her chest to keep her head from slamming the pavement. Sheer luck and good timing had her out the back before he could speed up enough to cause severe damage to her when she exited the vehicle.

Brake lights filled her vision as she looked back.

She heard him shift into reverse.

To keep reading, click here.

ABOUT THE AUTHOR

Barb Han is a USA TODAY and Publisher's Weekly Best-selling Author. Reviewers have called her books "heartfelt" and "exciting."

Barb lives in Texas—her true north—with her adventurous family, a poodle mix and a spunky rescue who is often referred to as a hot mess. She is the proud owner of too many books (if there is such a thing). When not writing, she can be found exploring Manhattan, on a mountain either hiking or skiing depending on the season, or swimming in her own backyard.

Sign up for Barb's newsletter at www.BarbHan.com.

Made in the USA
Middletown, DE
22 September 2021

48841722R00099